How Much Do You Love Me?

SHANKAR SAPRAM

To
My *Sati*

Contents

Chapter 1: Save Me with a Coffee

"Swirling across the wreckage of our bonding
I long for a tinge of elixir from your sensuous lips
To salvage my tormented soul from numbness;
'Cause no opium can heal hangover from our past,
Or will I be forever entombed deep in the rubble?
How long can I endure memoirs rumbling within?"

My intimate moment with the diary is interrupted by the opening strains of the song *'Jeena Jeena...'* playing randomly on the television. This song from *'Badlapur'*, which she often sang while reclining in my lap, swaying gently to its melody, floods my solitude with an unwelcome gale of memories. I hurry to the hall to stop it, leaving the diary on the bed. With my finger hovering on the remote's stop button, I struggle to press it immediately. It's not the melody that prevents me from stopping it, but the surge of memories triggered by the song. My racing heartbeat combines with the giddy and nauseous effect of the hangover—not from last night's drink, but from the intoxicating embrace of a six-year magical spell.

Till nine months ago, in the sanctuary of our living room, we whiled away countless hours, finding solace in each other's presence long into the night. Lost in each other's touch, we snogged for what seemed like an eternity, oblivious to the world around us. The gentle warmth of our intertwined hands, coupled with the soft rhythm of our breaths, enveloped us in a cocoon of intimacy. As beads of perspiration formed on my skin, the distant melody of the song stirred my senses. The same song now serves as a poignant reminder of her absence.

I can still vividly recall the tranquil image of her nestled against me, her rhythmic breathing a lullaby to my soul. The sofa, witness to our intimate encounters, seems to absorb and reflect the warmth of our love, its cushions imbued with the imprint of our shared affection. Each time I sink into its embrace, a flood of memories washes over me, painting the room with the hues of our past.

To elude every reminder of her, I decisively press the 'stop' button and then 'back,' seeking to change the song. Yet, the array of recommended thumbnails on YouTube stubbornly comprises her favourites or fragments of our erstwhile connection. Frustrated with a futile quest for something devoid of her influence, I have resignedly switched off the idiot box. The ensuing silence, suffusing the room, now acts as a catalyst for overwhelming memories to inundate my consciousness.

The air is heavy with the lingering essence of her presence, a delicate fragrance that permeates every corner of our home, wrapping me in a bittersweet embrace. The television, a silent observer of our love story, casts flickering flashes of light that dance harmoniously with the memories in my mind. Even the curtains, gently swaying in the breeze, seem to whisper secrets of our shared moments. It's as though she cast a spell upon our home, trapping me in the web of our memories, refusing to release me from the hold of our love. Compelled to take a breather from the suffocation of nostalgia, I flee the hall, seeking solace on the balcony accessed through the bedroom.

The rush of fresh air upon my senses is abruptly invaded by the pungent tang of cigarette smoke. Glancing around, my eyes are drawn to the sight of a striking young woman standing on the opposite balcony, her fingers delicately holding a long, white cigarette. Clad in a pristine white, full-sleeved shirt and blue jeans, her lips—rosy and creamy—are a captivating sight against the backdrop of the cityscape.

I find myself transfixed, anticipating the moment she brings the cigarette to her lips for a deep drag. Yet, she remains lost in thought, leaning against the wall without touching the cigarette to her mouth. Curiously, the image of a woman smoking captivates me, stirring a fascination that momentarily distracts me from my melancholic reverie. I light my cigarette, the flame briefly illuminating my face as I feign disinterest while discreetly stealing glances in her direction.

To my dismay, just as a young man emerges onto the balcony scene, she carefully hands the cigarette over to him, disrupting my fleeting fascination. The interplay of their interaction on the neighbouring balcony becomes a silent tableau against the backdrop of my turbulent thoughts, a bittersweet distraction from the weight of cherished memories that echo in the corners of my mind.

Disillusioned by my futile expectations of city girls in general, I turn away, attempting to savour the remnants of my cigarette. One of the most endearing aspects of our relationship was her willingness to learn to smoke just to please me. Whenever I sat on the balcony, she would join me, taking a puff or two, to grant me the sight of smoke escaping her naturally pink lips, a feast for my eyes. In the nine months since her departure, I've struggled to enjoy a solitary cigarette, her absence casting a shadow over even this simple pleasure. Perhaps it's time to give up smoking, too, another step on my journey to disconnect myself from her. Returning to the present from my trance, I drop the remaining half of my cigarette to the ground, crushing it underfoot.

Now, I find myself lying on the expansive double-sized cot in the bedroom, contemplating whether this space could serve as a haven of my solitude. We rarely spent time here, preferring instead to turn the living room into a bedroom and confining the actual bedroom to office duties. I would avoid intruding when she was engrossed in work on her laptop. But in her free time, she always gravitated towards me.

Suddenly, I sit upright, a pang of recognition coursing through me as her presence seems to endure in the very air of the bedroom. The closed windows only intensify her essence, trapping her fragrance within these walls. As I contemplate my next steps, the bedroom walls whisper memories of shared moments, the echoes of her laughter, and the warmth of her companionship haunting me.

My mobile screen lights up silently, signalling the arrival of a notification. I lift the device in my hands and find Instagram notifications waiting for me, the foremost one being a post from Priyanka, a close friend of hers. Knowing the allure and potential heartache that such notifications can bring, I make a deliberate choice to ignore them, fully aware of what to do to maintain my commitment to detachment. With a deep breath, I open the Instagram app and proceed to mute all posts and updates from Priyanka, understanding that some of her photos prominently feature my former companion. Despite the magnetic pull towards peeking at those images, I resist, taking the necessary steps to shield myself from the past.

As I navigate through my contacts list, muting those who might stir up memories of Her, I am flooded with a montage of poignant moments. Each name triggers a cascade of emotions, a tapestry of nostalgia interwoven with longing and resignation. The list seems endless, and a sense of desperation sets in. In a moment of impulsive resolve, I log out of my Instagram account, seeking reprieve from the relentless onslaught of reminders.

The mobile slips from my grasp and spirals through the air, crashing against the wall before coming to rest in a quiet corner of the bed. The impact echoes the tumult within me—frustration, longing, and the relentless pursuit of closure.

In the ensuing stillness, a realisation begins to settle. Some endeavours, it seems, are simply beyond human reach. To live a life severed completely from her feels like an insurmountable challenge. I find myself grappling with the enigma of her swift transition to happiness without me. How did I shift from being her entire universe, as she so often declared, to becoming a mere footnote in her life story?

Because it is accomplished by her, I am keen to know her secret behind being happy without me. I couldn't forget her tear-streaked face on our final encounter, who, by the evening, posed with a pout on her WhatsApp display picture. Meanwhile, my WhatsApp profile picture remains unchanged, a reflection of the darkness lounging in my heart long after she left.

The prospect of revisiting her profile fills me with dread. I fear discovering that I've been blocked, an indication of the irreparable abyss between us. Three months ago, during my last visit to her profile, I held naive hopes of encountering a sombre, soulful image as her display photo—a reflection, perhaps, of enduring sorrow. Instead, I was confronted with a vibrant family portrait, captured during a joyous outing. The contrast between her buoyant show and my own melancholy proved too much to bear.

Despite feeling a twinge of jealousy at her seemingly effortless strength of character, I cannot help but admire this trait in her. Who else could leave behind a fulfilling, six-year-long relationship and swiftly move on? When she was with me, I never even got the thought that she would one day walk away, abandoning our bond. We weathered numerous storms—fights, conflicts, and profound disagreements—yet our connection remained steadfast and unyielding.

Contrary to her assertions during our final encounter, it was often I who initiated reconciliation after misunderstandings. In the aftermath of our arguments, I would experience brief periods of despair, convinced that our relationship was irreparably damaged. Nevertheless, I would always be the one to bridge the gap, regardless of the circumstances that had led to our discord. I knew deep down that I could never bring myself to leave her.

We steered the challenging terrain of a long-distance relationship for two years, emerging from it stronger and more committed than ever. This achievement filled me with unwavering optimism, dismissing any doubts that might threaten our bond.

Yet, reality has proven far more challenging than my perceptions allowed. The nine months following her departure have been nearly unbearable. Within the first week, I was confronted with the stark realisation of who I was without her—the void she left within me painfully evident.

Her final communication—a curt email declaring her intention to sever all contact—echoes in my mind. I pored over that message repeatedly, searching for glimmers of hope, foolishly clinging to the notion of a potential reconciliation. It took time for me to acknowledge that I was chasing a mirage in the desert, my optimism a misguided attempt to stave off the inevitable.

The desire to reach out to her, to hear her voice directly, is a persistent temptation. Yet, I am haunted by her blunt honesty during our last conversation: "Your calls and messages are overwhelming. I cannot focus on my life with such a constant disturbance. Allow me the freedom to explore my destiny." Her words, though harsh, resonated deeply within me.

How could I possibly justify disrupting her newfound peace and freedom? The last thing I want is to become a source of turmoil in her life, overshadowing her pursuit of happiness and self-discovery.

It's a perplexing phenomenon, indeed, how a breakup can provoke such intense and sometimes violent reactions in individuals. The news is rife with stories of people resorting to destructive behaviours following the end of a relationship. While there may be various factors fueling this anger and despair, I often find myself questioning whether true love was ever present in these cases.

For me personally, I struggle to comprehend how love can transform into hatred, whether suddenly or over time. I fail to harbour any animosity towards her or to place blame for my current state of emotional dilapidation. Instead, I am inclined to examine my shortcomings and mistakes that may have contributed to our parting ways.

Even now, as I reflect on her treatment of me post-breakup, I am incapable of holding negative emotions towards her. My focus remains on seeking closure and moving forward without bitterness or resentment. If I were allowed to meet her again, the question that burns in my mind is simple yet profound: "How were you able to move on so swiftly, as though our time together never existed?"

Fatigued with the plethora of flashes from the memories filled duly with her, I decide to escape the haunting echoes by retreating from the bedroom. In that room, she would often work into the late hours of the night, leaning against me as I provided a steady presence for her. The weight of her back against my bent knees, a once-comforting gesture, now serves as a painful reminder of what once was.

Swiftly moving through the living room and into the kitchen, I find that I have been lost in thought, oblivious to the passing of time. The glow of my mobile screen illuminates the late hour—nearly ten o'clock at night. I recognise that I haven't prepared anything to eat, nor do I feel any appetite. However, out of a sense of obligation to sustain myself, I recognise the importance of providing my body with nourishment, especially to endure the impending, torturous night ahead.

Entering the small kitchen area to find something to eat, I search through the cupboards one by one. My hopes dim as I discover only a few expired items—packed potato chips, pastries, and other bakery products that have long passed their prime. Glancing at the long vertical shelf behind its transparent glass door, my eyes are drawn inevitably to the most perilous item in terms of my emotional commitment: a Davidoff Espresso '57 coffee bottle.

I've learned to be cautious, avoiding direct eye contact with it whenever I enter the kitchen. Despite this, I cannot bring myself to dispose of it. This bottle of coffee holds a profound significance—a history of shared mornings, the physical comfort of its warmth, the intimate chemistry of our interactions, and the intricate calculations of our togetherness.

With my steady gaze on the coffee bottle, I find myself unwittingly slipping into memories of our beautiful moments together, beginning with the earliest and most cherished—the day I first met her.

In my mind's eye, a torrent of vivid recollections floods over me, transporting me back to the flamboyant glimpses of our inaugural date. It was during a technical fest named '*Yuv Tharang*' hosted at her college campus. I had journeyed nearly fifty kilometres from my college, brimming with enthusiasm to participate in various events. However, my presentation was deemed redundant due to an oversaturation of similar concepts. Despite my lack of technical expertise, I was enlisted in the team for my exceptional stage presence and presentation skills.

As my friends embarked on a mission to persuade various panels to reconsider our topic, I sought solace and enjoyment in the main auditorium, immersing myself in the cultural events unfolding around me.

I made my way into the auditorium through a side entrance situated on the left of the stage, greeted by a packed crowd of attendees. The front rows appeared intentionally vacant, likely reserved for dignitaries or special guests. The hall itself was a spacious, circular venue, with rows of seats and desks arranged in a crescent shape, separated by a central aisle that led directly to the stage. The stage, positioned at the lowest level, rose upward toward the back of the hall, where another wide door marked the exit.

Standing near the stage entrance, I scanned the room for an available seat when suddenly, all the lights in the auditorium went out. In the ensuing darkness, a moment of magic unfolded before my eyes.

The rear door swung open, admitting a young female student, who quietly closed the door behind her. As she turned toward the stage, a series of lights above the aisle burst to life, casting a vibrant display of colours and patterns across the ceiling. Bathed in this stunning illumination, she began her descent down the aisle—a vision of grace and elegance.

Her attire—a crop-top lehenga adorned with maroon embroidery against a backdrop of deep beige—enhanced her curvaceous figure, accentuated by a freely hanging dupatta that billowed with each step like the regal attire of a princess. Despite the weight of her ensemble and the papers she carried, she moved forward with poise.

As she reached the third row, she engaged in conversation with another girl, her expression a mixture of earnestness and concentration. I found myself captivated by her celestial presence, my gaze fixed upon her until she reached the front row, where her search seemed to yield no results. Her large, expressive eyes betrayed a hint of frustration as she approached a faculty member seated in the front row, engaging in what appeared to be a brief but intense discussion.

Discontented, she made her way to the left side of the stage, standing before me with a palpable sense of urgency. Opening her papers under the dim lighting, she struggled to read, prompting her to rush to the electrician working at the amplifier on the stage's edge. Taking matters into her own hands, she began to practice reading from her papers, her head shaking helplessly, conveying her worry and apprehension.

At that moment, I felt a surge of empathy and determination. Despite our initial unfamiliarity, I was compelled to offer my assistance, driven by a desire to alleviate her distress and contribute to the success of her presentation. Being naturally outgoing, I summoned the courage to approach her, introducing myself and offering my assistance. Initially, she regarded me with scepticism, understandably cautious of a stranger's sudden interest. However, upon persistent inquiry, she eventually opened up about her predicament.

It turned out that her co-anchor was unexpectedly absent, leaving her to shoulder the burden of their joint presentation. She confided in me, admitting that she had practised a lesser part of the prepared script compared to her partner. On top of that, she harboured concerns about delivering spontaneous responses during the program, compounded by the absence of other volunteers busy with campus event preparations.

Eager to lend a hand, I shared my extensive experience managing stage productions at our college. In a matter of minutes, the script papers exchanged hands, a tangible sign of our newfound collaboration.

"Hi, my name is Saira," she introduced herself with a handshake, her demeanour shifting from apprehension to cautious acceptance.

It wasn't unusual for me to communicate and collaborate with girls, but Saira was different—special, even.

"I despise being part of the stage committee. Honestly, I'm more confident in my technical skills, but our HOD insisted on this role," she confided, her frustration evident.

"I clearly see the reason behind it. You, being a gorgeous beauty, must be a unanimous choice for an MC on the stage." I struggled hard to control my inner voice.

Her innocent demeanour, piercing eyes, and captivating fragrance—intensified by our proximity during our discussion—left a lasting impression.

Observing her throughout the program's commencement, I noticed her considerable fan base within the college community. Any doubts about my capabilities were swiftly dispelled as I took charge of welcoming guests to the stage with poise and precision. Saira visibly grew more confident as we progressed through the script, her initial apprehension giving way to a shared sense of accomplishment and purpose.

As the program unfolded, our collaboration blossomed into a harmonious partnership, fueled by mutual respect and a shared commitment to delivering a memorable event. Saira's charm and grace, coupled with my organisational acumen, laid the foundation for a successful presentation, bridging the gap between initial distrust and mutual admiration.

The program unfolded seamlessly, stretching out over nearly an hour and a half. Every passing minute felt like a cherished moment, the highlight of my life. I silently thanked fate for the missed opportunity of her absent co-anchor, allowing me to step into the role beside her that day. Throughout the event, we shared moments of conversation, getting to know each other, engaging in friendly debates, and sharing laughter.

As the event concluded with a vote of thanks, Saira expressed her gratitude and contentment, but I noticed a hint of weariness in her demeanour. Concerned, I inquired about her well-being, only for her to reveal that anxiety had kept her from eating since morning.

"Where's the cafeteria?" I suggested, eager to ensure she took care of herself.

"No, I really don't feel like eating," she declined firmly, catching me off guard.

"Don't I deserve a soft drink for all our hard work on stage?" I playfully countered.

"Oh, I'm so sorry. Let's go," she agreed cheerfully, her fatigue momentarily forgotten.

As we walked side by side towards the cafeteria, the weather seemed to mirror our mood, showering us with tiny drizzles and cool breezes that tousled her hair. It felt like a scene from a dreamy folklore romance, with nature itself setting the perfect backdrop for our companionship.

Along the way, I couldn't help but notice the admiring glances from passing boys, their eyes drawn to the gorgeous beauty beside me. Despite her casual conversation about college life, I found myself on cloud nine, too captivated by her presence to fully register her words. At that point, I entertained thoughts I'd once dismissed as myth—the notion of recognising one's soulmate upon meeting them. Now, I was convinced— I had encountered my soulmate in Saira.

"What would you like to have?" Saira asked me at the counter.

"Are you sure you don't want to eat anything?" I inquired, concerned about her well-being.

"I'm sure. I can't. I don't like soft drinks either in this cold weather. You take something, please," she replied.

"This is totally unfair. I won't have anything without you joining me," I insisted.

"Then what shall we do? We can have something hot instead. Shall we have a coffee?" she suggested.

Although I had never tried coffee before, I didn't want to disappoint her. "Yes, let's have it."

"Two coffees, please," Saira ordered and promptly paid the man thirty rupees.

In a few minutes, we found ourselves standing at an empty round table near a three-foot wall on the edge of the canteen, occasionally feeling drizzles splashing on us. Saira took her first sip and exclaimed, "Hey! It's not bad. This is the first time I'm having coffee in my life."

"The same is the case with me, too. I just wanted to have something with you, whatever its taste could be," I admitted.

She looked surprised. "Wow! What a coincidence!"

"How do you like it?" I asked.

"I think it will be a lasting taste," she replied with a smile.

As we relished the coffee together, I couldn't help but notice the curious glances from other students in the cafeteria, undoubtedly drawn by Saira's presence. Sensing my discomfort, she explained, "My college mates. It's the first time I've been in the cafeteria with a guy. It must be a wonder to them."

That day left an indelible mark on my life, a cherished memory that I hold close. However, I regretted not asking for her phone number, wanting to preserve the experience within myself. I kept our encounter private, treasuring every moment spent with her in the auditorium while allowing my poetic imagination to wander over how I could meet her again.

I eventually found her on Facebook, but fear held me back from sending a friend request, uncertain of the response I might receive. Time flew by, and two years passed. Through rare updates on her Facebook posts, I learned that she had relocated to Bengaluru, having completed her course. Without much hesitation, I decided to move to the same city, driven by an inexplicable pull towards reconnecting with the woman who had left an indelible impression on my heart.

Our second meeting occurred in a bustling coffee shop during the initial days after my move to Bengaluru. I was accompanied by two friends, still adjusting to the city's modernity and pleasant weather. We settled into a cozy corner, my friends playfully teasing me about my choice to forego any coffee. Meanwhile, they indulged in various flavoured cappuccinos.

Opting for a plain coffee without any added flavours, I wanted to immerse myself in memories of my time with Saira. As the waiter placed a tall cup of cappuccino adorned with a heart-shaped design in front of me, I immediately signalled him to correct the mistake, assuming it was meant for another table. To my astonishment, the waiter indicated that the order was placed by a girl from a neighbouring table—Saira.

At that juncture, I felt a rush of rejuvenation wash over me as if my life had just been reset, erasing all that had transpired before. Saira's unexpected presence felt like a reunion with a long-lost companion.

"I knew I would certainly find you again. Would you join me for a coffee, please?" Saira exclaimed, her words filling me with a sense of destiny fulfilled.

In the ensuing months, our bond deepened to a point where we couldn't bear to be apart, yet marriage remained out of reach for the time being. Saira secured a well-paying job, allowing her to live independently and support me financially. Coming from an affluent family, she could have easily afforded to live alone in a rented house, but what truly inspired me was her determination to earn her livelihood independently, without relying on her family's wealth.

She used to work from our flat at least two nights a week, spending the rest of her workdays in the office. Those evenings when she returned home, exhausted from her day, were the moments we both cherished most. As I made coffee for her in the evenings, it marked a time of day that brought us both immense happiness. My longing to see her would dissipate, and her desire to be near me would reach its peak all at once.

In the early days of our time together, she revealed a surprising fact—she hadn't had coffee again until she found me in Bengaluru. When I asked her why, she simply said, "I wanted to miss it intentionally." I learned that coffee served as a symbolic connection between us in two contrasting ways. She wanted to share it only with me, while I used it as a means to relive our memories whenever I wished.

As I find myself caught in a rush of memories, I inadvertently pick up the Davidoff coffee bottle. A surge of desire washes over me, craving a cup of coffee despite the commitment I made to myself. Without knowing it, I twist open the lid, and I'm immediately hit by the familiar aroma. But to my dismay, I recognise that the coffee inside has dried up, forming a hard precipitate at the bottom. I haven't opened it in months.

"Oh my god! What now?" I mutter to myself, overwhelmed by the sudden craving. "Is the corner shop open? I need coffee desperately."

As I hurry down the street, my mind races with memories of the times we shared over coffee, each moment etched vividly in my consciousness. The desire to recreate those intimate experiences has taken hold of me, driving me to seek out that familiar taste and aroma that once defined our togetherness.

I arrive at the corner store and dash inside, my eyes scanning the shelves in hopeful anticipation. The usual aisles seem unfamiliar, and the absence of my preferred coffee brand only intensifies my frustration. My heart sinks as I realise I will not find what I seek here. Despite being unfamiliar with this store's inventory, my desperation compels me to scour every corner, hoping to rediscover the essence of those cherished coffee moments.

As I comb through the store, the weight of my craving bears down on me, suffocating me in its grip. It's not merely about having any coffee; I yearn for the specific blend that carries the memories of our shared moments.

Disappointed and impatient, I storm out of the store, my determination unyielding. The world around me seems to blur as I contemplate my next move. The nearest shop that stocks the coffee we favour is a daunting 2 kilometres away, a distance that now looms before me like an insurmountable challenge.

I'm engulfed by a tumultuous state of mind, unable to comprehend my surroundings or the passing people who appear as mere blurs amidst the eruption of my volcanic craving for the aroma, taste, and essence of coffee that has been buried deep within my soul. The usual 2 km distance to the store feels like an endless trek, as my rising anxiety stretches time beyond recognition.

The troubled walk triggers vivid memories of her as if I'm being swept away by a colossal wave into an abyss. She permeates every direction, and I cannot escape her presence no matter where I look. Within me, two contrasting urges battle fiercely—one to revel in the heavenly beauty of her memory, and the other to resist succumbing to the addictive temptation of dwelling on her image.

Arriving at the store after what feels like an eternity, I am faced with a fundamental question: Is it coffee that I yearn for, or the love I once knew? The question lingers briefly before I rush inside the shop, seeking solace in the simple act of acquiring coffee.

At last, I locate the familiar bottle on the shelf, a beacon of hope amid the chaos of my emotions. With a sense of triumph, I grasp the bottle, feeling the weight of its significance in my hands. As I make my way back home, the anticipation of brewing that first cup fills me with a renewed sense of purpose.

Moments later, I'm back on the street, walking briskly with the coffee bottle in hand. Without hesitation, I unscrew the cap and tear open the wrapper at the top, releasing an enchanting aroma that not only awakens my senses but also stirs deep-seated memories. As I take in a deep breath, inhaling the aroma directly from the bottle, a flood of images rushes through my mind. I see her dancing like a fairy, moving to melodies inspired by our unblemished bond that was never meant to be tarnished.

In my hurry to return to the apartment and relish the celestial taste of the coffee, I am still enveloped in the memory of her graceful dance. This time, she dances alone, her ethereal form twirling and moving gracefully while I remain a mere spectator in the visual symphony of recollection.

Back in the kitchen, the anticipation builds as I wait for the water to come to a boil. Meanwhile, I indulge in the intoxicating fragrance of the coffee, each whiff stirring up memories infused with her essence. It's been nine long months since she left, and I've been avoiding coffee ever since, knowing that my attachment to her could lead to my downfall. But today, the craving is overpowering. I prepare the coffee with tender reverence, honouring the memories that infuse each moment with a poignant nostalgia. As I do so, I've absentmindedly selected her cup instead of mine. Despite their similarity, I can discern the subtle differences between the two, a testament to how deeply she has permeated my consciousness.

She was the one who taught me how to make coffee. The ritual begins with inhaling deeply the rich aroma that emanates from the coffee bottle immediately upon opening its lid. I became obsessed with the unique blend of coffee and her natural scent that enveloped us when we playfully cuddled in the kitchen. Her meticulous method of measuring out the ingredients precisely into our large cups never failed to fascinate me. As she swayed to a tune while humming to herself, the rhythmic movement of her hips and body left an indelible impression on me. Whenever I attempt to replicate her technique, those tender moments echo vividly in my mind. As I stir the contents in the cup, I can't help but remember the playful dance she taught me, where we'd rotate our bodies to a silent rhythm.

With the coffee now prepared, I bring the cup to my lips, eager to taste its familiar warmth. The first sip hits me like a wave, carrying with it a trace of her celestial beauty. The second sip follows quickly, then the third, each one invoking memories of our shared moments.

Revelling in the enchanting aroma wafting from each cup, we would take our first sips while gazing into each other's eyes. This act was invariably followed by a deep, passionate kiss that often extended into a prolonged embrace. With moist lips and loving looks exchanged, we would migrate to the balcony—the setting for our most cherished moments of the day. Sitting in our chairs, we would enjoy our coffee while recounting the day's events. For us, coffee time wasn't merely about hastily finishing the contents of our cups; it was a journey of sharing our worlds and expressing our love through wordless gazes into each other's eyes.

I continue to sip the coffee, each swallow drawing me deeper into the wellspring of our intimate moments. Suddenly, a precious memory rises to the surface like a gem glinting in the stream.

Once, during a coffee-flavoured kiss, she opened her eyes quietly after a long and tender exchange. Curious about her thoughts, I asked her what was on her mind. At first, she hesitated to answer, but upon my insistence, she revealed her heart.

"If there comes a day when I am away from you completely, even if it seems there's no hope for us to be together again, please remember that I still would want you to bring me back to our love," she said softly. "There's nothing that could separate us permanently, not even death."

The sensational revelation instantly opens my eyes wide, unleashing a rush of unspoken emotions within me. *"She's there waiting for me forever. She would never leave me. Nothing can diminish the heavenly bond we share. This coffee I'm having now—it's not just coffee; it's the key that unlocks my soul's relentless pursuit of her. Even though she was clear about leaving me forever, her true self always expects me to come for her, to try and fail in my attempts to reclaim our love. It's not a failure when I stumble while striving for the love of my life. I know I am nothing without her. She is everything to me, no matter where she goes or whatever circumstances she faces."*

I rush to the balcony, a place that has witnessed countless wonderful moments during our coffee times. For us, coffee wasn't just about drinking; it was a time to talk about everything, to argue, and to adore each other in many ways. With a surge of renewed optimism, I resolve to send her a message. As I pull out my phone from my pocket, I notice a notification from her email. Anxiously, I click on it to read the full content. It says, "Hi, I hope you're doing well. I haven't responded to your earlier messages because there's no point. I've moved on strongly, and I expect you to do the same. Goodbye!"

It is only now that I see things clearly. The repeated cycle of yearning for her companionship leaves me feeling empty once again. The attempt to reach out to her is futile, stirring up a multitude of memories that I had carefully kept dormant since she left me. How does one deal with a swarm of emotions suddenly awakened? Seeking refuge in the bedroom, I cover myself fully with a blanket on the bed, but each passing moment brings forth more perspiring memories from beneath it. I throw the blanket aside as I rise from the bed, feeling suffocated within the confines of my apartment.

Every inch of my living space seems to gnaw at me from within, compelling me to escape. I find myself on the terrace, leaning against a two-foot-high stunted pillar with my diary in hand, ready to pour out my despair onto its blank pages.

"How can I remain enveloped in our shared blanket, saturated with the remnants of our intertwined breaths? Despite dousing the bed and sheets with my deodorant spray, your aroma reverberates persistently. Removing the blanket does not offer solace; the bedroom itself is a repository of our romantic history. Should I retreat to the living room, each corner teeming with tales of our passion? The air still carries the vapours of our animated discussions on movies and

fashion, intertwined with memories of your graceful dances to Hindi melodies.

More than the oxygen my body inhales, it's the melodic tones of your voice, laced with a subtle huskiness, that quicken my heartbeat to the rhythms of our love songs. Every inch inside the flat bears witness to the layers of our unspoken conversations throughout our time together.

Stepping out onto the terrace, I seek refuge from your pervasive fragrance. Even here, the outdoors bears the imprint of our anniversaries, a testament to our deep connection. Yet, here I remain, under the open sky, hoping the breeze will carry away the atoms of our memories and bring in a breath of fresh air, allowing me respite for tonight.

Though the stars and ever-changing moon have borne witness to my sleepless suffering, I choose another night of restlessness outside, rather than being suffocated by our memories indoors."

I gaze up at the starlit sky, marveling at its divine beauty. Suddenly, it strikes me how the twinkling stars resemble the scene of Saira descending from the highest row of the auditorium, with a ceiling that seemed to celebrate her arrival like a celestial angel. Exhaling a series of smoke circles, I watch her imaginary descent from the sky through the swirling rings.

My eyes grow heavy, closing involuntarily as I sit with the unfinished lines in my lap, the pen dangling from my fingers.

Chapter 2: Longing

As I stumble out of bed, the remnants of last night's restless sleep cling to me like a heavy shroud. The familiar ache in my bones accompanies the dull ache in my heart, a constant companion in the wake of our parting. With a heavy sigh, I reach for my mobile phone, desperate to grasp some semblance of time in the ambiguous morning light filtering through the open window.

My mind feels clouded, and the memories of the night are still vivid in my half-conscious state. I struggle to piece together how I ended up back in the bedroom after my nocturnal reverie under the starlit sky. The image of Saira descending like an angel from the heavens reflects in my mind a bittersweet reminder of the love we once shared.

Blinking against the encroaching daylight, I manage to focus on the mobile screen, my bleary eyes squinting at the notifications waiting to be acknowledged. Among them, a reminder from Google Photos catches my attention—a memory from nearly three years ago, captured in a single photograph. In such a dozy state, I click on it to see the photo. This inadvertent temptation reminds me in the back of my mind about the need to reset certain settings in a few other apps, too.

Before I can fully grasp the mistake I've made, the screen displays a picture of us deeply kissing. The raw intensity captured in the image suggests it was taken by a third party, but I know it was my own hand that snapped the photo during that intimate moment. It's a scene I remember all too well—the transient bliss of an encounter in a Chennai airport transit hotel during a brief interlude in our long-distance relationship. Resisting the urge to ponder on the profound connection captured in the photo, I force myself to get up and toss the mobile onto the bed. However, unable to shake the feelings that have surged within me, I find myself reaching for the mobile once more as I step into the bathroom, memories of our two-year long-distance relationship flooding my mind.

"You take care of yourself, my love," she repeated with a heavy heart before she left, her tears staining her cheeks. "I curse myself for imposing this heartless punishment on you. Please forgive me. I wouldn't have accepted this offer if there had been an alternative. I don't want to leave you. Remember that you won't have me around to look after your health. See you."

Her words echoed in my mind as I watched her proceed through the security check at Bengaluru airport. For a moment, I forgot if I had existed before she entered my life —our lives intertwining so deeply that it feels as though we've always been together.

She was repeatedly wiping the tears off her cheeks. She didn't turn back until she disappeared beyond the security checkpoint. Her final goodbye wave, accompanied by a soulful gaze, imprinted itself on my memory, a scene I could still envision vividly.

As I stood immobile outside the airport, my mobile erupted with a flurry of notifications—messages from her, as I had anticipated.

"These two years, let's make them unforgettable by staying connected online," her words appeared on my screen.

"I never imagined a day that would take me away from you for this long and this far.

It's inevitable for the sake of our careers; I hope you understand.

This step will also delay my family's pressure to get me married.

Still, it feels more distressing than I imagined.

Even now, I feel like disembarking from the flight and running to hug you.

I pray that the onsite proposal to work in Abu Dhabi gets dropped by the client.

Sorry, I have to switch off my phone now; my eyes are too blurred to continue typing.

Lots of love and loads of kisses... See you, Shaanu..." One by one, her messages lined up.

I hastily typed my reply, my heart heavy with longing. "You always mirror my feelings, my love... See you, Saira!"

As I hit send, a deep ache settled in my chest, a silent companion to the void left by her absence. The days ahead stretched out like an endless expanse, each moment tinged with the bittersweet memory of our parting at the airport.

Knowing about her departure well in advance didn't fully prepare me for the profound impact it would have on my life. The day she left marked the beginning of overwhelming loneliness that I struggled to navigate during the initial month of her absence. Her departure seemed to erase any memory of my existence before she entered my life; her absence weighed heavily on my daily routines, thoughts, and overall sense of self. I realised I couldn't envision my life without her by my side.

Each day began with a video call, her genuine smile on the screen, infusing me with energetic positivity that carried me through the challenges I faced. Seeing her motivated me to strive harder for a successful career, as our future together relied heavily on our individual successes—a fact she often reminded me of during our conversations. While she was busy at work, I struggled to suppress the urge to constantly reach out to her, wanting to bridge the physical distance with our emotional connection.

Six months after her departure, she surprised me with the happiest news—she was planning a week-long trip to India on holiday. After securing permission from her manager and making the necessary arrangements, I felt elated, like I was on top of the world. Amongst the challenging times I was facing, including my gradual loss of interest in the IT field, her upcoming visit was a beacon of hope. I believed that meeting her again would not only bring immense joy but also help me rediscover my life's purpose. There were so many things I had kept hidden from our regular conversations and chats, waiting for the opportunity to share them with her in person.

To pile up my miseries, her trip was unexpectedly cancelled, as she informed me in an evening message after three days. Her family had organised a trip to Dubai and insisted that she join them. This news devastated me, and for the next three days, I found myself unable to communicate with her. Aimlessly wandering, my mind was filled with wild thoughts and fears that she might one day leave me for the sake of her large and prominent family.

During the ten days of her family holiday in Dubai, I found myself sitting idly in my flat, consumed by thoughts of her. I scrolled through the photos she sent on WhatsApp repeatedly without responding. She grew concerned when I didn't answer her calls, expressing how much she missed me and how every passing moment reminded her of our time together. Eventually, when I wrote, "You look amazing and your smile is as enigmatic as always.", she replied, "It was you whom I was looking at while the pics were taken. You are the glory in my eyes."

Fifteen days later, I was graced with the sight of her scintillating presence during a peaceful video chat, just as she always did when we were apart. After seeing her family off at the airport, she hurried back to her flat to connect with me over video. The longing in her eyes revealed just how much she had missed me during their visit. Despite the physical distance, we never truly felt separated, except when her family was with her. Our souls, filled with longing, delighted in every moment of the uninterrupted chat, which lasted for more than two hours. It's often assumed that couples in love might run out of things to talk about on repeated calls, but our connection was different. We never wanted to hang up, even after hours of conversation.

Six months passed by in a whirlwind of countless online episodes and frequent hiccups. One day, in the thick of a heated argument with my manager about appraisals, I made the impulsive decision to quit my job. I promptly submitted my resignation papers and ceased attending company calls. However, I lacked the courage to discuss this with Saira—not because I doubted her ability to understand, but because the decision unfolded so swiftly that I couldn't gather the courage to address it. I hoped to secure another job within two months, sparing me the need to disclose this episode to her.

During that period, I found myself struggling to meet my expenses while half-heartedly attending interviews for other companies. My inherent aversion to IT jobs was evident in my demeanour during these interviews, contributing to numerous failures. It became increasingly clear to me that it was time to alter the course of my destiny. I began to recognise my true self—a writer—struggling to emerge despite challenging circumstances. However, the most daunting aspect was how to broach this matter with Saira. She had consistently encouraged me to build a strong career that would meet her family's expectations when I eventually proposed marriage.

In truth, I lacked passion for the IT job, viewing it merely as a means to secure relatively high pay with minimal effort. Like many other young people at the time, I succumbed to the belief that achieving stability was straightforward and consequently gravitated toward it. As months passed, my authentic self yearned to break free from this mold. *"I am not cut out for this job; I need something more fulfilling in life."* This internal conflict between conforming to societal norms and pursuing personal fulfilment compounded with each passing month, adding immense pressure to my situation.

Then, two months later, in the dead of night, Saira awakened me with exhilarating news—she was *en route* to Malaysia via Chennai. Accompanied by her lady manager, she needed to attend a crucial meeting with their client, allowing for a five-hour layover in Chennai. She shared her flight details, urging me to plan our rendezvous for the day. Sleep evaded me amid this excitement, the scenario unfolding like a fairy tale beyond my wildest dreams. The prospect of seeing her again in person filled me with a mix of anticipation and nervousness, as I yearned to share my evolving journey and aspirations with her face-to-face.

I was in Bengaluru, yearning to reach Chennai by flight to meet her at the airport. Researching all possible ways to spend private time together, I was drawn to the idea of a transit hotel, which offered privacy without requiring us to venture into the city. A colleague suggested that transit hotels were ideal for short and intimate stays, albeit costly. He mentioned it would cost around eight to ten thousand rupees for a 3-hour stay. Considering the expense, I calculated that my round-trip flight between Bengaluru and Chennai for the day would amount to eight thousand rupees alone. With additional expenses for refreshments throughout the trip, I estimated needing around twenty thousand rupees. However, I was nearly penniless at the time.

As I planned my trip to meet her at Chennai airport, the weight of my recent struggles and joblessness weighed heavily on my mind. I knew I couldn't face her until I disclosed this part of my life. Determined, I composed a meticulously thought-out message, akin to drafting a cover letter for a job application. It felt strange to write to her in such a different tone, but it was necessary. After reviewing it repeatedly, I finally mustered the confidence to send it just as she boarded her plane in Dubai. I cursed my usual hesitation, knowing it had caused an unnecessary delay.

Waiting anxiously at the arrivals gate in Chennai airport, I couldn't help but repeatedly check for the single tick indicating the message had been sent on WhatsApp. Part of me was tempted to delete the message before she read it, fearing it might spoil the moment of our reunion after so long. Elation, anxiety, fear, longing, love, self-pity, and self-motivation clashed within me, each vying for dominance. Emotions ran wild, and my mind was filled with a whirlwind of thoughts.

Restless, I sat alone with a cup of coffee, gazing at the arrival lobby and checking the time, despite knowing her flight had yet to land. Finally, the announcement of her flight's arrival sent my heart racing. I had never felt such fear and anticipation in her presence before.

After a long half-hour wait, I caught a glimpse of her emerging from the left turn at the far end of the arrival lobby. She strode briskly toward the exit, pulling her trolley behind her, engaged in a last-minute conversation with her manager. Despite this, her beautiful eyes were searching for me in the crowd. As soon as she bid farewell to her manager, her gaze found me instantly, and her eyes lit up with a radiant smile that reassured me everything was well.

We hurried toward each other, and upon meeting, she instantly took my hands in hers. It was a touch that conveyed her ownership of me, a feeling I had missed for many months. At that moment, I realised she hadn't read my message yet. Suddenly, I felt a pang of regret for sending it that day. I thought to myself, *"I should have disclosed everything after this meeting. What a foolish mistake I've made. It might spoil the good time she was looking forward to."*

We navigated through the bustling airport lobbies, our eyes locked in a silent exchange of joy and anticipation. Arm in arm, we ventured into the lift that would take us to the floor where the transit hotel awaited, following the clear signs guiding our way. A contagious smile played on our faces, reflecting the unspoken excitement and intimacy of a newlywed couple seeking private solace.

Surrounded by the noisy crowd, our eyes spoke volumes, conveying a deep connection and understanding that surpassed words. Her happiness radiated through her eyes like never before, a testament to the pure love she felt at that moment. In return, I felt a profound sense of contentment, knowing that our silent communication mirrored our mutual feelings.

'This is all I want,' I thought to myself, soaking in the shared joy and affection that enveloped us as we ventured closer to our private sanctuary.

We approached the front desk of the transit hotel, where a young woman greeted us with curious anticipation. As we requested a suite, she promptly began checking her computer, scanning our flight tickets with a hint of surprise.

"Are you two travelling together?" she inquired, noting the different flight details on our tickets.

"Yes, we are together. We need a room for both of us," Saira responded confidently.

"But your flights are different. You're not travelling together based on these itineraries," the woman pointed out, her suspicion evident.

"That's correct. My husband came to see me off, and he will return to his destination later," Saira explained, emphasising our relationship.

The woman's doubt persisted as she inspected our tickets again, raising an eyebrow in uncertainty.

"But you're not even from the same place," she noted with growing suspicion.

"That's true. Is there a requirement that transit accommodations are only available for travellers from the same place or on the same flight?" Saira retorted, her impatience mounting.

"No, it's not like that, but I..." The woman hesitated.

"Could you please check if there's a vacancy? We're tired after travelling, and it would be helpful to know," Saira pressed, her tone becoming more assertive.

The woman relented, presenting us with a price list that outlined rates for stays ranging from a minimum of three hours to twenty-four hours.

After taking copies of our IDs, the woman swiftly entered our details into the booking system. In a couple of minutes, the process was completed, and an attendant was ready to escort us to our room. He led us down the corridor, showing us the way, and introduced us to the unique features of the room before leaving.

The room was somewhat cramped, centred around a large bed with minimal space on either side. Saira placed her trolley in a corner and took my bag to store it alongside hers. She removed her black jacket and casually tossed it onto the luggage before stepping closer to me.

Finally, after what felt like an eternity of waiting, we found ourselves in a secluded, private space. Standing opposite each other, we gazed deeply into each other's eyes, each of us captivated by the other's presence. She looked extraordinarily beautiful, her features illuminated by the soft, dim light of the room, casting a gentle glow around her.

Inevitably, drawn by an irresistible force, we closed the distance between us and became united in a soulful kiss. Our lips moved together in a dance of passion and longing, each movement filled with the intensity of our feelings for one another. The world outside seemed to fade away as we lost ourselves in this intimate embrace, relishing every moment of closeness.

After a while, we slightly tilted our heads to allow for necessary breaths, the quiet room punctuated by the synchronised rhythm of our exhales amid the lasting warmth of our kiss. My arms held her tightly, feeling her embrace me just as deeply as if trying to merge our souls through this connection.

As we continued, our lips and tongues moved in a harmonious exchange, a language of desire and affection spoken between us. My hands, guided by a mixture of passion and tenderness, explored her body, tracing the curves and contours beneath her clothing until I felt the soft touch of her skin beneath her garments, a sensation that filled me with a sense of completeness and longing.

For the first time in a long while, I felt truly whole, enveloped in her intoxicating scent that seemed to persist in the air around us. Her natural fragrance enticed me further, pulling me deeper into the moment we shared. The taste of her lips was pure and untouched, a testament to the fact that she hadn't eaten anything. Despite my realisation, I couldn't bring myself to break the kiss, nor did she show any intention of stopping. We continued, immersed in the blissful union of our souls, cherishing each second as if time had stood still for us alone.

"You haven't eaten anything," I murmured after what felt like an eternity, my gaze fixed on her reddened lips, evidence of our passionate exchange.

"Neither have you, except a coffee," she replied with a sigh, her voice filled with shared longing. Taking my hand in hers, she guided it down to her trousers, positioning it just outside her damp panties. As I felt the warmth and moisture, I looked at her affectionately, overwhelmed by the intensity of our connection.

Gently, I pressed against the fabric, my touch eliciting a soft response from her. Eventually, I withdrew my hand, pulling her into a passionate embrace, my lips finding her forehead in a tender kiss.

"Your touch alone is enough, Shaanu," she whispered, her voice barely audible but filled with emotion. As I met her gaze, her eyes brimming with unspoken feelings, I couldn't resist leaning in for another soft, sweet kiss on her lips, our hearts entwined in this intimate moment.

We savoured the fruit salad she had brought in her handbag from the plane, a testament to her thoughtfulness and care that always set her above me. As I enjoyed the flavours, I couldn't help but marvel at her ability to anticipate my needs and desires—wishing I could match her in this regard. From my bag, I produced a strawberry smoothie, a special treat I had picked up for her outside the airport. The delight in her eyes and the warmth of her embrace when she saw it confirmed how much she appreciated the gesture.

The next two hours unfolded as some of the most cherished moments we had ever shared. She nestled comfortably in my lap, her voice a soothing melody as she spoke freely about her life in Dubai—her experiences, aspirations, and dreams cascading like rain in a monsoon. My fingers traced gentle circles around her nipples, the fabric of her black bra offering tantalising resistance now and then. In that intimate setting, time seemed to suspend itself, as if life had paused to honour this precious juncture where I felt immensely fortunate to witness her genuine joy and openness. Each passing moment was a treasure, etching itself into my memory as I basked in the beauty of her uninhibited self-expression.

The wake-up call from the reception rudely interrupted our intimate moments, serving as a harsh reminder of our impending departure. With a sense of reluctance, we hurriedly attended to our basic needs and freshened up. As we readied ourselves in ten minutes, Saira expressed a desire to capture a memory of our time in the room. She suggested taking a photo of us kissing, a proposal that initially caught me off guard but quickly grew on me.

Not particularly skilled in taking selfies, I fumbled through multiple attempts to capture the authentic moment she envisioned—real, unscripted kisses that conveyed our genuine connection. Each try brought us closer to achieving the desired shot. Finally, we achieved a snapshot that encapsulated the essence of our fleeting moments together, a memory she promptly transferred to her phone for safekeeping.

As we arrived at her check-in counter, aware that her flight was scheduled to depart in two hours, Saira briskly completed the necessary procedures. Standing together at the security check, we acknowledged that this was the moment of parting. I couldn't accompany her further as my domestic flight required me to proceed to the gates on the opposite side.

It was during this bittersweet moment that Saira broached the topic of my job situation. I was taken aback to learn that she had been aware of my resignation for two months.

"Yes, I found out the first Monday after you resigned," she revealed. "You can't hide anything from me, Shaanu! I noticed a change in you from that day onwards. I was waiting for you to bring it up during our meeting here, but you messaged me before landing. You can't face me while hiding something."

Her words resonated with a mixture of understanding and concern, underscoring her perceptive nature and the depth of our connection. Despite the challenges we faced, her unwavering support and intuitive understanding offered a sense of comfort in the middle of the uncertainties.

I stood there in silence, absorbing her words, my eyes fixed on the depth of her gaze that spoke volumes of sincerity and understanding.

"The key to success lies in recognising your skills early," she continued, her voice a blend of encouragement and honesty. "I admire your self-awareness. Some people struggle to find their path even at 50. But let me be candid with you. When I introduce you to my family for a marriage proposal, I want you to stand as a successful person. We face other challenges, particularly in our community, where acceptance of interfaith relationships is not easily gained. I stand by you in all things, but I ask that you achieve a stature they cannot dismiss."

Her words resonated deeply within me, and I couldn't help but feel overwhelmed by the weight of our situation. Tears welled up in my eyes involuntarily. We shared a heartfelt hug before she had to leave, tears mingling with our embrace. I felt the warmth of her touch and the wetness on my chest from our shared emotions.

When I lifted her head to meet her eyes, I noticed the tear tracks on her cheeks. My own eyes were on the brink of overflowing with emotion, each blink threatening to release another wave of tears. She wiped her cheeks as she moved through the security queue, stealing glances back at me that tugged at my heart.

As she gradually disappeared into the crowd beyond the security check, she became a blur, leaving behind an overwhelming sense of emptiness. I stood there, grappling with a profound feeling of loss.

Minutes later, overcome by emotion and weighed down by the pain of separation, I turned and made my way towards the domestic check-in counter. Throughout the process of boarding my flight, tears threatened to spill again and again, accompanied by an increasing sense of suffocating pressure.

I couldn't recall the specifics of how I navigated the check-in counter, passed through security, or found my way to the departure gate. Even upon receiving her departure message, my eyes remained clouded with tears. She had sent me a picture from inside the aeroplane along with a message that read, "Miss you *ra,*" followed by a red heart. I knew she must have been feeling the same emotions, but perhaps she composed herself in the presence of her boss or for my sake. The picture only reinforced the ache of separation, a reminder of the distance between us.

With the vibrant echoes of memories still dancing through my mind, I gradually emerge from the depths of reverie into the blurry reality of the present moment. The persistent nudges from my colleagues succeed in pulling my passive presence back from the ocean of reminiscences. As I realise I'm seated in the office cafeteria, a fog lifts from the events of the past hour.

As informed by my colleague, during the past hour, I was in an online review meeting with the client, my team lead (TL), and the manager in the conference hall. Owing to what felt like a whirlwind of intense moments, I struggled to address certain issues raised by the clients, much to the frustration of my superiors. Their mounting anger eventually led to them physically pushing me out of the conference room, their voices drowned out by the flood of memories consuming my mind.

Now, sitting alone in the cafeteria, I find myself lacking the courage to approach them and explain my current state. I yearn to convey the truth about how I've been merely existing, consumed by the unrestrained flow of thoughts and memories of Saira that blur the lines between reality and dream. I ponder, "How many times will they forgive me for my destructive behaviour in the project?"

Helplessness settles over me as I sit together with my colleagues, feeling their pitiable gazes directed my way. None of them truly understands the turmoil within me.

"I need you, Saira! Truly, I am nothing without you," I whisper inwardly, longing for the solace and strength that her presence once brought into my life.

✳ ✳ ✳ ✳ ✳

In the late evening, I find myself at a nightclub with my colleagues, seated on a solitary bar stool at a quiet table, observing the dance floor and the random people around me. Every girl's presence inadvertently brings thoughts of Saira flooding back to me, making it difficult to see anyone else without thinking of her. As I immerse myself in this silent reverie, Karthik, my colleague friend, approaches me with a sense of helplessness evident in his expression.

"Things happen in life, and we need to move on," Karthik remarks, attempting to offer words of consolation. I struggle with conflicting feelings—part of me is frustrated by what feels like a mundane and impractical lecture on responsibility, while another part is grateful to have someone attempting to console me at this point of distress. The mention of "moving on" instantly triggers memories of Saira's email urging me to do the same, momentarily causing me to withdraw from the conversation.

"Why aren't you drinking anything?" Karthik asks, clearly vexed by my indifference.

I take a moment before responding, "You need to understand the situation and focus on the work. All the team members are here to support you and figure out what's bothering you," Karthik explains further, his frustration palpable. "You were well-trained and performed adequately during the interview—that's what the TL told me. Until a few months ago, your contributions to the project were solid. We're struggling to understand what's changed recently. What's going on with you? Please consider the impact on our team if we fail to deliver the project on time.

Your cooperation is crucial for its success. Do you understand?"

Meanwhile, the other five team members sit at another table under the soft, twinkling lights of the nightclub, awaiting my response and hoping for a breakthrough in my demeanour.

I reflect on Karthik's words, feeling a mix of guilt and resignation. How could I explain to them the weight of memories and emotions that lingered from my relationship with Saira? The pain of her departure and the struggle to move forward without her overshadowed everything else. Each day felt like a battle against myself, and facing the expectations of my colleagues only added to the burden.

Enclosed by the pulsating music and lively chatter of the nightclub, I feel disconnected from it all, lost in a sea of unresolved emotions and inner turmoil. Karthik's voice fades into the background as I retreat further into my thoughts, grappling with the realisation that I must confront my own demons before I can fully engage with the world around me again.

Vishal's frustration boils over in a cacophony of sharp words, the noise of the nightclub momentarily silenced by his outburst. "Are you out of your mind? Just drink it and let the shit out of your system. We have no patience to witness your drama for the whole night," he exclaims, his voice cutting through the dimly lit atmosphere.

His words hit me like a sudden jolt, and I feel a wave of pity wash over me for causing such disruption to the camaraderie of the group. Despite their insistent gazes demanding an explanation, I remain silent, unable to articulate the depths of my emotional turmoil.

Finally, gathering the courage to share, I open up quietly, my voice barely audible over the pounding music. "I only drink with her," I admit, the weight of my words hanging in the air amidst the puzzled looks of my friends.

"It's a commitment I made to myself," I continue, my voice gaining a bit more clarity. "I only find joy in socializing and drinking when she's with me. Before Saira entered my life, things were different. I used to enjoy these gatherings, but now... everything has changed."

As I speak, the rawness of Saira's absence reverberates within me, filling me with a profound sense of emptiness. "I'm terribly sorry, guys," I add, my voice tinged with regret. "I'll do my best to focus on the project, but I can't enjoy these moments without her. Please carry on without me."

The group's reaction is mixed—some are staring at me with pity, while others express frustration by abruptly leaving their seats. I watch them depart with a heavy heart, feeling the weight of my emotions bearing down on me.

In a sudden burst of excitement, Dinesh strides over to us with a curious gleam in his eyes. He places a hand on Karthik's shoulder and points towards a young woman amid a lively dancing crowd at the far end of the hall. Intrigued, Karthik follows Dinesh's gaze and asks who she might be.

"Don't you recognise her? Try to place her. Haven't you seen her before?" Dinesh's voice is laced with intrigue and excitement. Karthik remains uncertain, his eyes scanning the group of youthful dancers. Dinesh persists, "I haven't met her in person, but I've definitely seen her around."

A spark of recognition lights up in Karthik's eyes as he turns to Dinesh for confirmation. "Is that Kalyani, the latest sensation known as the 'Bengaluru Techie' on Pornhub?"

"Yes, that's her," Dinesh confirms eagerly. "Whenever I watch her videos, my body and mind crave her. It's astonishing how we missed recognising her, considering she's from our city. She's absolutely captivating."

I remain silent, my expression betraying my lack of familiarity with the subject. Karthik promptly retrieves his phone, opens the browser, and enters the same keywords Dinesh mentioned moments ago. A series of websites populate the screen, and Karthik selects one, leading us to a video featuring the same girl in a close-up shot, her expressions hinting at an intimate experience.

Uncomfortable with the explicit content, I urge Karthik to close the browser. Together, we navigate through the bustling crowd towards her. As we approach, Dinesh's voice rises above the music with anticipation, "Longing for a night with you, my sexy lady!" and turning to me, he asks, "Is your flat free tonight?"

Chapter 3: Penance

I find myself walking alone on the rain-soaked road, surrounded by vehicles speeding through the downpour. The raindrops sparkle under the city lights, creating a mesmerising spectacle in all directions. Two hours ago, when I left the pub, I was asked to spend the next few hours outside before heading home. With no specific plan in mind, I decided to embark on the five-kilometre journey back to my flat on foot, hoping that the walk would help pass the time and perhaps wash away the memories that weighed heavily on my mind.

As I traverse the city streets, the LED signs on the main road add to the vibrant atmosphere, their bright displays illuminating the otherwise dark night. Now, having turned onto quieter streets, I am greeted by the soft glow of intermittent yellow streetlamps. The pattern of these lights serves as a reminder of the nights spent with Saira, our hands intertwined beneath a shared umbrella, exploring these same streets together.

The rhythmic sound of our footsteps splashing in puddles at street corners echoes vividly in my mind. Each puddle we crossed brought a refreshing coolness to our feet, countered by the warmth of our shared breath during tender moments beneath the umbrella. Despite the rain now soaking my face and lips, I can almost feel her touch and taste her presence in the air.

With each turn onto a new street, the romantic ambience intensifies. The gentle yellow glow of the streetlights casts a soft, dreamlike hue over the falling drizzle, evoking memories of our intimate moments together. Yet, as I continue to relive these memories, it becomes increasingly challenging to maintain composure in such a romantically charged setting. Each street corner holds echoes of our past encounters, making it difficult to reconcile the present with the lingering sensations of our shared experiences.

It is the dead of night, and here I sit upon one of the sturdy concrete structures positioned in the open expanse beside my flat on the terrace. The prescribed two-hour wait has yet to elapse, and so I remain outside. The rain persists, though not as torrential as before—rather, it's the customary Bengaluru rain, a gentle drizzle that tickles the senses. Initially, I sought shelter close to the walls under the extended roof, but the allure of the cold wind, accompanied by occasional showers, drew me out. I find solace in the open space, relishing the warmth of the rain as it brushes against my skin.

The closed windows continue to reflect the indoor lights, indicating that my colleagues are still inside. A pang of devastation washes over me as I contemplate the private space that was once shared intimately with Saira, now being tainted by the illicit desires of my colleagues. Yet, in a peculiar twist, I find myself entertaining the notion that such unholy acts might serve to cleanse the unwanted memories tied to her. Since her departure, no other woman has graced the flat—a testament to the sacredness of our shared space. Could this sanctity be further compromised by my indulging in impure actions?

"Do I need to defile myself to purge her from my mind?" The sudden vagary strikes me as oddly sensible. I have always upheld honesty and fidelity to her memory. Perhaps it's time to explore the opposite path—adulterate myself to a point where I no longer deserve her. Maybe then, the relentless stream of her memories will begin to recede.

My introspective moment, with closed eyes facing the sky, is abruptly interrupted by the increasing intensity of raindrops splashing on my face. This sensation triggers a vivid flashback of a shared moment in the bathroom shower, where both of us stood beneath the cascading water, eagerly awaiting the first droplets to fall on our faces. The memory washes over me, momentarily transporting me out of my thoughts.

All of a sudden, a strong urge to behold her image overtakes me, and my hands instinctively reach for my phone in my pocket. To my dismay, I recalled that it was switched off hours ago and safely stowed away in a polythene cover during my rainy stroll. With my mobile—a repository of our cherished memories— now out of battery, my fleeting chance of solace is lost in a mirage.

I find myself standing at the cliff of my uncontrollable obsession, yearning to see her images. Despite my efforts to move forward and distance myself from her, in moments of weakness, I am drawn back to see her images again with an irresistible force. Countless times, I've contemplated deleting all traces of her from my phone, yet I lack the courage to follow through. I remain unable to suppress this rising desire to see her, to talk to her, even if only through the lens of her photograph.

Now, having lost all hope of immediate comfort, I am left to conjure her presence from the deepest layers of my memory by projecting her divine smile onto the screen of my mind's eye.

From the innocent snapshots capturing her playful antics to the elegant images of her in a saree, a kaleidoscope of memories floods my mind for tens of minutes. Surprisingly, the sheer volume of these mental images far exceeds what was ever stored on my mobile device. Among them are my captures of her during casual outings, formal occasions, and intimate moments—all securely preserved within a special mental folder behind my closed eyes. Whenever I shut them, she materializes, vivid and tangible.

It's not merely the quantity of these mental photographs that astounds me, but the enduring fixation of my eyes on her presence. If only eyes possessed the remarkable capacity to store memories independently, what a curious sight that would be! I acknowledge now the rationale behind glimpsing her on the rain-soaked road, an impossible occurrence made plausible by the persuasive nature of the mind's eye. The mind obediently follows the eyes' lead, embracing an exotic and unexpected dominion of vision over thought.

Each mental image that unfolds is impeccable in detail, capturing every nuance of her beauty, down to the subtle mole on her chin—a feature that might go unnoticed in ordinary photographs. The precision of my eye-camera renders additional lighting effects unnecessary; her natural radiance shines through effortlessly. Meanwhile, the soundtrack of my undying love for her serves as the perfect accompaniment, enhancing the emotional depth of each remembered moment.

Lost in this immersive reverie, I'm instantly pulled back to reality by a husky female voice, disrupting my internal slideshow. Opening my eyes, though the mental imagery persists, I find myself face-to-face with a woman leaning against the wall beneath the roof. She holds a cigarette in her left hand, the wisps of smoke gracefully rising upward. Her face, adorned with full makeup that shimmers in the dim light, gradually comes into focus.

It dawns on me that she's Kalyani from the pub, taking a solitary smoke break. Offering me a cigarette, she playfully remarks on my trance. "Hey, young saint!

What are you looking at with your eyes closed?" Her observation about my constant eyelid movement and peaceful smile evokes a sense of gentle amusement, as if she's witnessed a serene infant during tranquil sleep.

"I'm… I'm trying to sleep," I reply, drawing closer to her to accept the cigarette.

"Out here, in the rain? Are you still thinking of her? Your friends told me that you're struggling with post-breakup depression."

"What is that p…p…post…?" I stumble over the unfamiliar term as I take a puff, sensing a different flavour mingling with the smoke—her lipstick. It had been ages since I tasted anything like it on a cigarette, especially from someone other than Saira.

"Forget it. They say you're suffering, but you seem to be in a different state of mind altogether," she observes, her tone tinged with curiosity.

Once again, I fall silent.

"You must have loved that girl so deeply that her memories transport you into your own world, oblivious to everything around you. The yogi-like posture you're in, lost in hours of deep meditative focus on your love—you're no less than a true mystic in penance. You're certainly undergoing a penance, my dear!"

"I didn't know I was in such a posture. I was just recalling her images stored in my active memory.

That's my way of willingly tuning out the world and living in her universe," I explain softly.

Returning the cigarette after a few puffs, I study her beautiful face adorned with scattered droplets of drizzle, reflecting the distant twinkling lights. Her glossy lips, slightly smudged makeup, and the way she holds the cigarette between her fingers exude a sensuous and seductive aura. Clad in a transparent saree that slightly reveals sumptuous displays on her waist and just enough cleavage to captivate any man, she emits an enticing allure. The wisps of smoke curling from her heavenly lips fuel my wild thoughts about adulterating myself.

Lost in contemplation, I realise my colleagues inside would gladly offer me an opportunity if I asked, viewing it as a gateway to vent my emotions. Perhaps such an outlet would help increase my productivity at the office.

"But can I really do this with her?" A weighty contemplation envelops me, drowning out the chaotic whirl of my thoughts. *"Can I truly empty my desolate soul and indulge my physical desires with this woman, who has already been embraced by so many others? Even if I succumb to this extreme act, can I ever be absolved by the part of myself dedicated to Saira? I doubt it. Why do these reckless thoughts persist? Disregarding the consequences, am I capable of initiating this intimacy with her?"*

"What's on your mind? Do you want something?" Kalyani's sarcastic grin snaps me back to reality abruptly.

"No, nothing. I'm just soaked in the rain. But I can't go inside right now, can I?"

"Why not? It's your room, and they've arranged for me to be here tonight just for you. I'm willing to do whatever it takes to break the spell you're under. Come on in." She strides towards the main door, tossing aside her cigarette butt. I trail behind, watching her exposed back as we enter the flat.

Inside, the hall is empty, and the bedroom door is shut.

"Are they in the bedroom?"

"It's fine. They're sleeping now. They won't mind if we use this space," she says, drawing closer to me.

I shift uneasily on the sofa, trying to create some distance between us. Kalyani then settles beside me, the first woman other than Saira to share this space, which slightly unnerves me. In the confines of the closed room, her presence is accompanied by a unique fragrance—a blend of her deodorant and her natural scent—that subtly captivates my senses. As Kalyani slowly leans in close, her face mere inches from mine, her warm breath brushes against my skin. At this moment, her seductive whispers and proximity awaken desires that have long been suppressed.

"I can't help but admire her beautiful and curvy body," I confess to myself, struggling to control my thoughts. *"How did this lady end up becoming a prostitute? Could the video clip on the adult website provide answers to my questions?"*

"Let her memories be overlapped by our fresh indulgence. She chose her way out of your home. Can't you allow yourself to gratify your special needs?" Kalyani murmurs, her words carrying a hint of persuasion. I remain conflicted, torn between my longing for intimacy and the deep-seated loyalty to Saira that still anchors me. As Kalyani's lips draw closer, my mind races with uncertainty and hesitation. The room feels charged with anticipation, a battleground between my physical desires and my sense of fidelity.

"An inch before is an opportunity to cast myself away from her shores forever," I reflect silently, grappling with conflicting desires. *"Kalyani's proximity presents a temptation to relinquish myself from the burden of memories tied to Saira, to unshackle my soul from the weight of her presence in my life. Should I make myself undeserving, unworthy even to entertain thoughts of her, in hopes that the incessant rain of moments shared with her might finally cease? Yet, the notion of polluting my body, tarnishing my physical being as I have done to my flat, pains me deeply. I've resisted turning my home into a den of indiscretions, refusing to stain the monuments of love and joy that once filled these walls with Saira.*

How then can I contemplate compromising my very self?

Or perhaps I'm simply overthinking, second-guessing myself instead of seizing the chance to revel in the allure of this beautiful, seductive woman who offers herself to me so willingly?"

I slowly step back, distancing myself from Kalyani, and rise from the sofa. As I walk toward the window, she watches me closely with curiosity.

"Please go into that room, lady!" I assert, my voice firm.

With a smile tinged with expectation, Kalyani complies, moving toward the opposite window. Then, unexpectedly, she reveals, "There's no one else in the house except us."

Perplexed, I respond, "What? Where are my colleagues? They were the ones who brought you here, right?"

"Yes, they brought me here, but now they are at the police station," Kalyani explains calmly, observing my worried expression. "Don't worry! They'll be back tomorrow morning. No charges will be filed against them; they're just being questioned for some information."

My expression remains puzzled as I urge Kalyani to continue.

"The main reason I accepted their offer to come here was because of you," she begins. "They told me it was to help get you out of the difficult time you've been having since your breakup. The other reason was that they had the MC with them and offered to share it with me, bragging about it. Little did they know that I'm also a secret informant for Mr. Bhasker, the CI of our area. He's actively tracking drug peddling in the city. As part of my work, I visit people in person and frequent pubs on my own, and any trace of the MC will be reported to him."

I am left utterly flabbergasted by her revelation.

"They were taken into custody just a few minutes ago, and the police will release them in the morning if they provide proper information about how they obtained the item," Kalyani explains further.

I take a moment to process this unexpected turn of events before asking, "If your job here was done, why didn't you leave?"

"I wanted to meet you because I'm intrigued by your devotion to the girl who left you months ago," Kalyani admits. "I'm greatly impressed by your detachment from other ladies like me. When you moved back from me just now, it showed your true saintliness. It's not easy to maintain that level of devotion for long. I don't know how much longer you'll be able to withstand the turmoil within you. Either the intense emotions will overwhelm you and lead you down a darker path, or you'll come to accept reality and move on. This transitional phase cannot last indefinitely."

I listen quietly to her insights into my life.

"Are you certain nothing will happen to them at the station?" I ask, concerned.

Kalyani reassures me, "Look, I'm thinking of you, and you're worried about them. That's just who you are. They'll be back home in the morning. The CI won't give the peddlers a chance to catch wind of anything."

It gives me a quick sigh of relief.

"Can I stay here for the night? I want to soak in the atmosphere of this place a little longer," she asks me, her eyes hopeful.

As she speaks, memories and thoughts swirl through my mind. *"All that happened here was love, passion, and desire,"* I reflect silently. *"The intention behind it might make this space holy forever. I didn't share those moments with her for any personal gain."*

"Yes, please stay," I reply warmly. "Would you like to sleep in the bedroom? This sofa is comfortable enough for me."

"That's great. Good night then. It's already late," Kalyani responds, a soft smile gracing her lips. "Wipe off your head and get some rest."

"Sure. Good night," I reply, feeling a mix of emotions.

"By the way, I'm Kalyani," she adds, extending her hand in a friendly gesture.

Surprised by her openness, I smile back and extend my hand to shake hers. I watch her with admiration as she walks gracefully into the bedroom, leaving me to reflect on the unexpected turn of events.

"I wonder how the connection works between physical cravings and the soul," I muse quietly to myself as Kalyani disappears into the bedroom and I settle on the sofa. *"I understand that it doesn't happen with strangers."* Reflecting on the proximity with Kalyani, I contemplate the complex relationship between physical desire and emotional connection. *"A body should yearn for union when the soul truly longs for the other,"* I realise. *"When she came close to my lips, it was Saira whom I envisioned with closed eyes, despite the strong fragrance that surrounded me."*

I acknowledge the challenge of replacing memories, understanding that overlapping experiences with someone new don't erase the past easily. *"Her fragrance will certainly live on, perhaps replacing the impactful scents that currently surround me, if not from my mind,"* I conclude, contemplating the intricate interplay between memory, desire, and emotional attachment.

*****

As the clock strikes eight in the morning, I awaken from my slumber, wrapped snugly within a blanket. The usual dimness of my apartment is replaced by the gentle glow of sunlight filtering through the windows, casting warm rays across the room. It's a sight that catches me off guard, as I'm not accustomed to such brightness in the early hours. Glancing toward the slightly open bedroom door, I catch the faint sound of a news channel playing on Kalyani's mobile phone. The broadcast brings news of heavy rains that lashed our city, Bengaluru, overnight—a stark contrast to the usual soft, romantic drizzles that characterise Bengaluru's weather.

Exiting the comfort of my blanket, I step outside to assess the aftermath of the storm. The scene that greets me is striking: rain returns gently, enveloping everything in a shimmering veil. The streets below are transformed into shallow rivers, rainwater pooling up to three feet deep. I can only imagine the plight of those living on the ground floors, potentially stranded in their homes. It's a moment that underscores the practical challenges we face—chief among them, what to eat in this watery chaos.

As I step into the kitchen, the warmth of the stove and the comforting smell of cooking fill the air. Kalyani stands before the stove, focused on her task, her movements deliberate and efficient. Beside her, I notice a pack of bread and two eggs, ready to be transformed into a simple yet satisfying meal. Watching her work, I'm struck by the contrast between this scene and the memories of Saira in this kitchen. Saira, with her gentle demeanour and occasional culinary surprises, used to bring a sense of celebration to our meals. Her presence stays in the corners of my mind, intertwined with the sounds and scents of everyday life.

Leaving Kalyani to her cooking, I step away and head to the bathroom. The familiar space offers a moment of solitude, yet it's also a trigger for memories of Saira. The bathroom becomes a sanctuary for reflection, a place where memories of Saira come flooding back. The memories bring a bittersweet pang to my heart, a mix of longing and appreciation for the moments we shared. Despite the passing time and physical distance, Saira's presence remains palpable, woven into the fabric of everyday life, even as I listen to the sounds of Kalyani's cooking in the present day.

As I enter the hall, I find Kalyani comfortably seated on the sofa, engrossed in the news playing on the TV while enjoying her meal. Seeing her contented state brings a sense of happiness.

"Yours is there on a plate in the kitchen," she replies casually, not taking her eyes off the screen.

"Did you make it for me, too?" I ask, slightly surprised by her thoughtfulness.

"Yes, of course. How could you think I'd be so selfish as to only cook for myself?" Kalyani jests, her tone light and friendly.

"I'm just concerned about your meal," I clarify, a hint of warmth in my voice.

"Come on! Get it here," she encourages, making room for me on the sofa.

Fetching my plate from the kitchen, I join Kalyani on the sofa. As I take the first bite of the egg sandwich, I'm pleasantly surprised by its exquisite taste, prompting me to look at her with admiration.

"This is delicious. I'm impressed," I remark, genuinely pleased by the unexpected culinary delight.

"You don't need to thank me. I have a request instead. Can I be your guest for today in your flat? The rain doesn't seem to be stopping anytime soon, and the roads are flooded," Kalyani explains, gesturing toward the TV where images of flooded streets and heavy rainfall flash across the screen.

"You can definitely stay. I don't have much planned for the weekend, whether it's rainy or not," I assure Kalyani, considering the unexpected company with a hint of curiosity.

"Are you a fan of Bollywood movies? The suggested videos on YouTube seem to imply that," she asks, her tone curious.

"They were more her favorite than mine. I've actually avoided watching TV for the past six months," I respond, diverting my gaze toward the elegant saree draped across her.

"Do you like wearing sarees? It's quite unusual to see someone of your age in one, unless you have a special interest in them," I inquire, intrigued by her choice of attire.

"Yes, I absolutely love wearing sarees. It's something I've fantasised about since I was a child. I couldn't wait to grow up just so I could wear one, you know?" Kalyani shares, her eyes sparkling with nostalgia.

"That's so endearing. I can see the childlike enthusiasm in your eyes," I remark, genuinely touched by her explanation.

After a brief pause, I continue, "I find it hard to believe myself sitting here with you on this sofa. The only woman I've known is Saira. I know I can't move forward unless I let go of her, but I'm finding it difficult," I admit, acknowledging the attachment to Saira that seems to colour my interactions with other women.

This internal resistance, devoted to Saira, subtly emerges as I sit beside Kalyani, making it challenging to see anyone else without the shadow of Saira loitering in my mind.

Kalyani heads to the kitchen after finishing her meal, and I swiftly devour the last two pieces of the sandwich, washing them down with water. As I approach the kitchen, Kalyani, already washing her plate, asks me, "Do you have any of her dresses left in the flat? I badly need a shower, and I can't repeat the same saree."

I stand nearby, waiting for my turn to wash, but she swiftly takes my plate before I can respond. "It's okay if you don't want to give me her clothes," she adds casually.

I know there are a few of Saira's tops lying at the bottom of the wardrobe in the bedroom, but the thought of Kalyani wearing one of them sends a surge of apprehension through me. I've been careful since Saira left, not to see or touch her clothes, wary of stirring up memories that last for days. Allowing Kalyani to wear one of Saira's tops would feel like deliberately disturbing a beehive, inviting unwanted thoughts and emotions.

"I'm sorry, but I don't have any spare dresses to offer," I respond, trying to push away the memories flooding my mind. "However, I can lend you some of my clothes. Would that work?"

Kalyani looks at me, seeming relieved. "That's fine. Thank you," she replies with a smile.

Having no other excuse to offer, I reluctantly venture into the bedroom cupboard to retrieve a pair of tracksuit bottoms and a relatively new t-shirt. As I rummage through the clothes, I deliberately avoid laying eyes on a particular folded t-shirt tucked away at the bottom of the pile. I dare not touch it, as it holds memories of exchanges with Saira that I am not yet ready to confront. The vivid flashes of our past moments threaten to overwhelm me, but I manage to evade them long enough to emerge from the bedroom with the garments for Kalyani.

Handing over the pale blue tracksuit and dark blue t-shirt to Kalyani in the hall, I am met with an instant smile. "You seem to have stopped ageing at the high school level," she remarks playfully. "It reminds me of school uniforms."

With a soft chuckle, Kalyani retreats to the bedroom for her bath, closing the door behind her. Almost immediately, the power fails, leaving me alone in the dim light of memory-laden silence.

An hour passes before the sound of the bedroom door handle jolts me from my reverie. Kalyani emerges, her hair cascading freely as she wipes it with a towel. Covered in the tracksuit and t-shirt I have provided, she looks entirely transformed. It is remarkable how magically clothing can alter a woman's appearance. Though I find her stunning in a saree, the loose t-shirt and oversized tracksuit bottoms seem out of place on her not-so-chunky frame. The contrast of her golden complexion against the dark t-shirt is striking, but the tracksuit bottoms trail awkwardly around her feet as she struggles to move gracefully, a reminder of someone else's presence that I can't shake off.

"Finally, I have someone to share my weekend with," I whisper to myself, observing Kalyani's tentative movements in the flat as she adjusts to her new clothes. It's unintentionally endearing to watch her navigate the space, and I find myself feeling a sense of companionship that extends beyond the physical presence in the flat—it feels like I have someone in my life again.

"It's just like me being in a drought all these months and suddenly getting cold showers on my hardened soul," I reflect silently. *"At least you have someone here around you to speak with. Why do you still talk to yourself?"*

As I observe Kalyani settling into the environment, her presence brings a subtle shift in my demeanour. Despite my inner dialogue persisting, I'm drawn to the idea of engaging in a real conversation. But can I truly allow myself to let go of the past, or am I simply seeking temporary solace in the company of another?

Kalyani continues her search in the refrigerator, and I listen to the clinking sounds emanating from the kitchen.

"Have you found what you're looking for? The fridge is mostly empty these days. I'm not really into cooking, even for myself," I remark, approaching her.

"I've managed to find a few vegetables hidden in the corners. Let's see if we can whip up some lunch with these. We can't go out in this weather," Kalyani replies, assessing the contents she has unearthed.

"You're right. This unexpected downpour in Bengaluru is quite something," I concede.

"Don't worry. I've found three types of vegetables. We can make sambar by combining them. Thank goodness you have onions. Where's the tamarind?" she inquires.

"It's in the white box with the other condiments beside the stove," I answer, retrieving the tamarind. "There's not much left. Will this be enough?"

"It's more than sufficient for today. And do you have any papads?" she asks.

"Of course, you'll find papads in every bachelor's home," I chuckle. "We're saved for the day."

"Do you know how to make sambar?" I ask hesitantly. "I usually stick to basic curries and haven't ventured into more complex dishes like sambar."

"Leave it to me. I'll handle the cooking, and you can assist me when needed," she reassures me.

"Absolutely," I agree, feeling a sense of relief at the prospect of having a meal prepared by someone else for a change.

"What about her? Your love?" Kalyani's question cuts through the mundane atmosphere, venturing into a realm of my life that has remained largely unspoken of for a long while.

I pause, my heart quickening at the mention of Saira. "She's quite different from me. More interested in cooking, always experimenting with new dishes when she has the time. I, on the other hand, stick to the basics," I respond, my tone quick and tense, trying to suppress the flood of memories her name evokes.

As we continue working together in the kitchen, an hour passes in shared camaraderie. It strikes me deeply that Kalyani is the first person in a long time with whom I've spent such candid, companionable time. In the middle of cooking, I find myself imagining what it would be like to have a true friend like her by my side, someone who could help me break free from the clutches of the past. Yet, I temper my thoughts with the realisation that it might be too fanciful to hold onto such hopes. The fleeting nature of our encounter brings a sense of melancholy, acknowledging that she may not stay long, and we might never cross paths again.

As Kalyani receives a call and gestures for me to finish cleaning up in the kitchen, I am reminded of similar nonverbal cues from Saira whenever she spoke with her parents. It's remarkable how even these subtle gestures evoke memories of someone I've been trying so hard to forget. I always admired the trust Saira's family placed in her, never doubting her, even when she stayed with me privately in the flat. I recall the day she introduced me to her mother as just a colleague from the office, unaware of the deep romantic relationship we shared. That introduction marked the beginning of my struggle with her family's unwitting involvement in our separate lives.

During the initial days of our parting, I used to respond to Saira's mother's calls and messages, trying to maintain a semblance of normalcy in our interactions. However, each conversation only served to reignite the undying feelings I had for Saira. Her mother would speak about her daughter's life, unknowingly complicating my efforts to move on.

Eventually, I decided it was best not to respond at all, fearing that any engagement would deepen my attachment to Saira, hindering my progress in letting go. It's a delicate balance between honouring the past and embracing the future, one that often leaves me feeling torn between loyalty and self-preservation.

Kalyani returns to the hall after her call and relays the news. "Your friends were released this morning. The police had other pressing matters to attend to, so the CI forgave them without much questioning. They've taken down their details for future reference. Do you think they actually had drugs with them?"

"Last night was my first outing with them," I respond, reflecting on the events. "I had no idea what they were planning. They mentioned they were willing to share what they had, promising to lift me out of my personal hell and introduce me to ultimate pleasures. But then they encountered you."

As I recount the previous night's events, a mix of relief and concern washes over me. The sudden turn of events and the involvement of law enforcement highlight the precarious nature of the company I keep.

"It's time for us to have our lunch. Our special guest today has prepared a sumptuous meal," I declare.

"Special guest?" Kalyani questions.

"Yes, indeed. I haven't had any guests here for many months. You can see the flat hasn't been properly cleaned. I've hesitated to disturb the memories as I tidy up. Just give me a couple of minutes, and I'll arrange our lunch."

With that, I fetch two small stools from the corners of the room. Taking an unused towel from the shelf, I spread it over the small table formed by joining the two stools. Meanwhile, Kalyani brings the food from the kitchen and places it on the table, one dish at a time, as I arrange the water.

Kalyani prefers to keep the window in the hall open, enjoying the ambiance with intermittent drizzles. In more ways than one, she reminds me of Saira, particularly in her admirable qualities like cleanliness. Kalyani even cleaned the hall while I briefly showered in the bedroom a few minutes ago, surprising me with the hall's unusual tidiness upon my return.

We sit down to eat, positioned across from each other. I've fetched a chair for Kalyani while I settle on the sofa. The drizzles occasionally brush against us as the wind sweeps through, adding to the pleasant atmosphere as we dig into the sambar she prepared. The crispy fried papads perfectly complement the hot, flavorful liquid. Lost in the enjoyment of the meal, I fail to notice how quickly I'm devouring it, my focus solely on satisfying my cravings.

Pausing momentarily to glance at Kalyani, I catch her watching me with amusement. We exchange smiles, and I resume my rapid eating, not realising how absorbed I've become in my meal. Kalyani breaks the moment with a witty remark, gently holding my plate with my left hand.

"Slow down and leave the plate. It won't run away," she quips, eliciting more smiles between us as we continue enjoying the delicious food together.

⁕⁕⁕⁕⁕

"Can I light it here?" Kalyani asks, cigarette between her lips and lighter in hand, seeking my permission. We're leaning against the window, entranced by the raindrops distorted by heavy winds outside. Smoking indoors was never our habit when we were together; it was always on the balcony or the open area beside the flat.

"The odor of this smoke might help wash away the pungent fragrance of my past from the flat," I perceive, and so I give her a slight nod of approval. She lights the cigarette and takes a deep first puff.

I watch in fascination as she exhales a large cloud of smoke through her lips. *"What a delight it is to watch this lady releasing a huge puff of smoke through her juicy lips,"* I think to myself. *"Has she come here to wipe out the unwanted stuff from my life, or to replace the past with fresh tunes of joy and new realms of happiness? Is it even possible to think of wiping out completely?"* My mind's wandering continues.

"What are these circles?" Kalyani notices something on the window edge—circles of rust formed by keeping something there constantly.

"Two circles on the two corners. What used to be here? I observed them when I cleaned it a few minutes ago," she says.

"They are remnants of two flower pots. She loves plants, especially indoor ones. She kept two of her favorite plants in the pots, and she used to give them a lot of attention," I respond hesitantly.

"Oh, that's wonderful. She must have kept names for the plants. Hasn't she?" Kalyani inquires.

"Yes, you are absolutely right. The names are 'Happy' and 'Soul'."

"She has taken both of them from me—my soul and happiness, which I had when she was with me. What remains here is a mere wasteland," I feel like saying it aloud.

*****

One week has passed, filled with relatively productive work at the office. I've been keenly aware of the impact my personal struggles have had on my team members, prompting me to make a conscious effort this week not to burden them further. Amid the daily routine, thoughts of Kalyani have frequently infiltrated my mind, accompanied by wavering doubts and curiosity about who she really is.

As the weekend approaches, I find myself grappling once again with the familiar challenge of loneliness and uncertainty about how to spend the next two days. Friday night unfolds in a haze of reminiscence, the memories of Saira playing out like a bittersweet reel in my mind. I lose track of time as I dwell on the moments we shared, the laughter, the warmth, and the ache of her absence.

As Saturday dawns, I wake to the weight of solitude, uncertain of how to navigate the empty hours ahead. The weekend stretches out like a vast expanse, inviting introspection and a tinge of restlessness. In this liminal space between past and present, I am left grappling with memories that refuse to fade and a future that remains uncertain.

"Calling someone first by myself has never happened in my life, and why would it happen now with someone I've only known briefly? I'm definitely not going to call her," I murmur to myself on the idea of inviting Kalyani to my flat for the weekend. The weekend feels daunting for those without many friends. A friend once pointed out that the amount of happiness in one's life is proportional to the number of friends they have, and I've come to understand the truth in that statement since Saira left. In her company, I never felt the need to befriend anyone else. My whole universe revolved around 'Saira'. When old friends reached out with messages, I bluntly ignored them, now recognising it as my sheer vanity. I was so stubborn that I isolated myself, convinced that I had the everlasting companionship of my life. Now, if I could advise young people, I would urge them to cultivate many friendships alongside committed

relationships. When the partner leaves, as is inevitable, it's true friends who can pull you out of the depths of depression. Unfortunately, I'm not fortunate in that regard to emerge from this abyss.

Finishing my breakfast, I settle onto the sofa, hoping to distract myself from thoughts of Saira by watching TV. I choose a thriller movie, expecting to avoid any romantic storylines. However, I quickly discover the plot revolves around a young girl and her lover, prompting me to stop the movie and curse the filmmakers for not creating a film devoid of romance. I switch to Netflix in search of something else, only to realise that our subscription has expired—an expense Saira usually managed. She was always the one to handle financial matters, taking care of everything we brought into our home, from the fridge to the sofa and TV. With her financial support, we never felt like bachelors living together; we saw ourselves as a married couple, making decisions and planning together. Our home was always a shared space. The way we lived together couldn't have predicted the barren loneliness I now face. This destiny was never on our horizon.

The quest to find a suitable movie that aligns with my current state of mind stretches on for the next two hours, each attempt ending in disappointment. As lunchtime draws near, I decide to abandon the pursuit of entertainment and turn my attention to cooking, viewing it as a meditative activity that will occupy my thoughts and energies.

Entering the kitchen, I am met with the familiar remnants of her presence, but I am determined to inject a sense of creativity into my culinary efforts. Surveying the contents of the refrigerator, my eyes settle on the vibrant red tomatoes, triggering a flood of memories associated with her homemade tomato *rasam*. The vivid recollection of her endearing video, filmed exclusively for me during our long-distance relationship, resurfaces. I can still envision her alluring expressions and hear her sweet voice narrating the cooking process, which resonated not only in my ears but also in the depths of my heart.

In the midst of the flurry of memories, a poignant question emerges: *"How could she leave all that behind and move on?"* This question reverberates within me, leaving me grappling for answers and struggling to chart my own course forward, bounded by the reverberating echoes of our shared past.

Chapter 4: "Happy Birthday"

"I don't know why I'm writing this, but it seems to be the only way to release the relentless waves of emotion I still hold for you. It has been eleven months since we parted, and I've only recently discovered that writing is a powerful way to ease my anguish."

I aspire to be a writer, and my thoughts always turn to Saira when I think of what to write about. That's why I'm composing this excerpt, of course, in the diary.

"I've been struggling to accept your departure, finding it hard to regain control over myself. I constantly remind myself that I mean nothing to you and you are happier without me. I'm trying to keep my distance from you to avoid causing you any disturbance, but paradoxically, the further I push myself from you, the more you loom large within me.

After much consideration, I've concluded that the best way to express myself without bothering you is to pour out my feelings onto paper.

Many times, I've contemplated deleting all the contacts linked to you and your friends from my phone, hoping to shield you from any emotional turbulence that might arise within me like a tsunami. Yet, I can't bring myself to remove your mobile number. The mere thought of losing that connection fills me with a deep sense of loneliness, and I fear it might drive me to the brink of madness. Despite this, I know that merely having your number doesn't equate to wrongdoing on my part.

Whenever I pick up my mobile, the overwhelming urge to call or message you immediately takes hold. Struggling to resist this impulse, I'm then met with the desire to at least see a photo of you somewhere on my phone. It might sound extreme, but I find myself consumed by thoughts of you constantly, battling to suppress them all. This struggle has led me to distance myself from my phone these days, keeping it at arm's length because I lack control.

Even when my phone rings, which is rare in a day, I remind myself not to open any messaging apps like WhatsApp. It's a constant internal conflict that plays out within me.

This morning, upon waking up, my first instinct was to check if you had responded to my earlier messages. How foolish of me! After many days, I've started checking my phone every two minutes for your messages. Although none have arrived, I can't seem to stop checking every five minutes. What baffles me is how I maintain such unwavering optimism about receiving a response from you, even when the chances are low.

As I write this, I catch myself repeatedly glancing at my phone for your replies. It's as if I'll never fully comprehend my own actions and emotions.

I often wonder how swiftly you managed to detach from our relationship and emerge so strong and seemingly unaffected by our past. I want to make it clear that I'm not blaming you; rather, I admire your resilience and self-assurance in navigating our issues and moving forward successfully. Many times, I've wanted to ask you the same question: How can I escape this ongoing cycle of self-destruction without causing you any distress? However, I hesitate to reach out because I fear disrupting your newfound happiness with your family, as evidenced by your various profile pictures depicting joyful moments. How could I possibly disturb your peace? I would never want that.

Lately, I've come to acknowledge that my own distress is impacting those around me. I find myself becoming irrationally angry over trivial matters and immediately regretting my behaviour. Despite repeatedly urging myself to be kind and considerate, I continue to behave in ways that hurt others. I'm uncertain about what those around me must think of me. However, I'm keenly aware that there's no one looking out for my well-being or mental health.

Speaking of health, I've recently experienced a peculiar issue where my body has refused to accept any food. About two weeks ago, I suffered a severe episode of this refusal and was unwell for five days, necessitating saline treatment through intravenous drips. While lying in bed connected to saline, I couldn't help but feel foolish for thinking of you and hoping that you might think of me occasionally.

During that time, I refrained from looking at your photos or attempting to message you because I feared that expressing my emotions could lead me to reach out to you again. That's the last thing I want, as I'm determined not to disrupt your peaceful and contented life.

I don't deserve you, and I never blame you for leaving me to face my own fate. Instead, I shoulder all the responsibility for our current circumstances. I know I made mistakes, and you endured them for six years. Ultimately, I must have done something unforgivable to drive you away. Throughout our relationship, you used to tell me that you couldn't bear the thought of us being apart. Now, it seems you're content leading your life without a second thought for me. Meanwhile, I feel lost, with nowhere to turn and nothing to occupy my thoughts, like a lifeless body awaiting the end. However, I want to reassure you that suicide is not an option—it's a crime and the gravest of sins. Please don't worry about that.

During those six years, whenever I closed my eyes to pray, thoughts of you would fill my mind. I prayed for you then, and I continue to do so now. Since I'm not sharing this writing directly with you, I feel I can confess that I observe fasting on Fridays, solely wishing for your success, happiness, and well-being. I *understand it's an important day for you, and I intend to pray for you selflessly.*

I've noticed a shift in my spiritual outlook. The boundary between my devotion to the Almighty and thoughts of you is slowly fading. As a result, I've stopped looking at religious symbols or idols. I no longer pray in temples or recite traditional mantras exclusively for the divine. Instead, I chant the name of the Almighty alongside yours, with equal intensity and frequency. However, I refrain from closing my eyes before religious icons because doing so instantly brings thoughts of you to my mind.

I'm uncertain if this approach could be considered blasphemous, but for me, it feels like a form of penance. Every breath I take has become a prayer, blending my devotion to the divine with thoughts of you."

As I write and immerse myself in memories of her, I feel intoxicated by the deliberate unveiling of emotions in my diary. Suddenly, I crave coffee to take a physical break from my thoughts. I head to the kitchen, spoon some coffee into my cup, and then close the Davidoff bottle. As I return it to the shelf, my eyes catch the expiry date printed on the bottle: 'Aug 2024'. The word 'August' momentarily stops my mind in its tracks, as her birthday falls in that month. It's as if a swarm of bees has been unleashed, buzzing with thoughts and plans for her upcoming birthday.

In an instant, wild and crazy ideas that have lurked in the shadows of my consciousness begin to reveal themselves, suggesting numerous ways to honour and celebrate this sacred day.

It's foolish of me to think that an external trigger is necessary to bring her birthday to the forefront of my memory. This occasion is significant and should be inherently present in my thoughts. Despite my efforts to push it aside, reminders of her birthday seem to permeate every aspect of my day. Whether I'm taking a bath, riding to the office in a cab, having coffee alone at work, or smoking a cigarette at a nearby café, her birthday inevitably surfaces in my mind.

Although I often deny its significance, there are moments of weakness when I entertain the idea of wishing her on her birthday. *"Should I reach out and wish her?"* This question relentlessly confronts me, leading to internal debates that extend to mentally drafting an email for the occasion. Although the content of the draft is concise—no more than four sentences—it absorbs my attention entirely, shielding me from everything and everyone around me while I contemplate this internal dialogue.

As August approaches, the internal turmoil intensifies, urging me to decide whether or not to wish her a happy birthday at all costs. However, as a self-defence mechanism, the most painful memories resurface: her last words spoken in the ice cream parlour during our final meeting, the harsh words penned in her last email, and her tearful plea not to disturb her during our last audio call. These memories reinforce my resolve not to disrupt her life, even if it means refraining from wishing her on her birthday.

Interestingly, there aren't any extraordinary memories associated with her birthdays, aside from her adorable poses in photos taken with unfamiliar friends. It's almost miraculous that none of her birthdays were celebrated in my presence during our six years together. As I write this, a sudden jolt of memory astonishes me—I realise that our first kiss occurred on her birthday. Despite the sweetness of that memory, subsequent birthdays were marred by unwelcome experiences. My indifferent attitude towards birthday celebrations clashed with her high expectations for the day. There was even a disagreement preceding one of her birthdays, which fortunately resolved on the day itself. In retrospect, I don't blame her for feeling hurt; she deserved to feel special on such an important occasion, and my absence undoubtedly caused her pain.

Bounded by the tumultuous emotions and the persistent inner debate about whether or not to reach out to her on her upcoming birthday, I find myself seated at a quaint roadside café. It is that tranquil hour just after office hours, with the evening sun casting a golden hue over everything around me. I seek solace in the routine of lighting a cigarette, a small comfort amidst the disarray of my thoughts. Yet, the wind is unusually fierce that evening, thwarting my attempts to kindle the flame with my matchstick.

At that moment of frustration, an unexpected company arrives. A pair of hands gently join mine around the matchstick, and as I look up, I am surprised to see Kalyani—the only other woman I have encountered in my life—standing beside me. She approaches with an air of familiarity, her presence both unexpected and strangely comforting.

I take a long drag from my cigarette, the smoke mingling with the swirling breeze. As I glance at Kalyani, her appearance is striking; she is draped in a vibrant saree adorned with shades of red and black, her makeup impeccable, and her posture poised.

In a surprising gesture, she extends her hand towards my cigarette, silently requesting a drag. I hand it to her, intrigued and mesmerised by the unexpected encounter. Watching her take a deep, confident puff, I find myself captivated by her graceful demeanour, momentarily distracted from the weight of my own thoughts.

"What brings you here, saint?" Kalyani's extroverted nature surfaces instantly as she joins me at the roadside café.

"Here... for a smoke. You know that I live nearby," I reply, my attention still fixated on her as she smokes.

"I've thought about you often, my pure gem! I've always wondered about your relationship with smoking," she remarks casually.

"I've wondered too. Some things stick with you even when you don't intentionally seek them out," I respond cryptically.

"Philosophy, my friend?" she asks, her tone playful.

"Perhaps from a confused soul," I admit, surprised by my own candour. Sometimes, you feel compelled to share with certain people, even if they're not traditionally close to you.

"Confusion for a soul as pure as yours? That's hard to believe," Kalyani remarks, returning the cigarette after a few puffs. Her gesture triggers a flood of memories that has jolted my sluggish consciousness.

Taking the cigarette back from her is a significant act for me. Sharing a smoke with a lady is a rarity in recent times, almost akin to a direct connection. Uncomfortably, my mind flashes to the only other woman who had shared a smoke with me, her image vivid in my mind's eye.

"To do or not to do, that is the question," I muse aloud.

Kalyani responds with reassuring conviction, "Everything done by a pure soul like you is a good deed. There's no question about it. Just do it. Your intentions can never be malicious."

Her words spark a surge of hope and solace within me. *"When intentions are pure,"* I reflect internally, *"actions naturally become positive and beneficial for everyone. No one has ever proclaimed this to my troubled soul."*

Lost in my thoughts, I sense that Kalyani is speaking again. "Has he gone somewhere again? Let me finish this before you come back," she remarks casually as she moves to sit on a nearby bench. Instantly, another man vacates the spot to stand at a distance.

Kalyani seems unfazed by the slight, enjoying her cigarette with indifference, and turns towards the other direction. The scene unfolds before me, a curious and unexpected interlude in my otherwise introspective evening.

"Meeting you here has cleared my mind in many aspects. You are truly gifted, I believe. I don't know how much I should thank you," I express to Kalyani, grateful for our unexpected encounter.

However, my expression of gratitude is abruptly interrupted by the ringing of my mobile phone. A wave of concern washes over me when I see it is my mother calling.

"It could be some kind of financial emergency at home," I think anxiously as I answer the call, only to hear someone else's voice on the other end. My face gets darkened as the brief conversation unfolds.

Kalyani, noticing the worried expressions on my face, asks me after the call if my mother is alright.

Struggling internally, I have shared with her that my mother fainted earlier in the afternoon and was rushed to a nearby hospital.

"I must go to her at once," I declare, my urgency evident as I prepare to leave. The unexpected news has cast a shadow over our brief encounter, but Kalyani's presence and concern have left a lasting impression on me.

Reflecting on the years of my personal happiness and the subsequent traumatic aftermath, I discover that I completely neglected my mother. I visited her rarely because I didn't want to leave Saira alone. While I did call my mother regularly, I didn't respond well to her repeated requests for me to come home more often. In the fog of those years, I failed to truly listen to her during our conversations, often just waiting for the calls to end quickly.

After Saira's departure, I found myself unable to make calls at all. I didn't want to burden my mother with the knowledge of my deteriorating state. I needed to stand on my own feet before facing her again. The phrase "taking for granted," which Saira often used with me, accurately reflects how I treated my mother. This realisation unsettles me deeply.

As my mind races with chaotic thoughts, Kalyani shows immense kindness by arranging a train ticket for me to travel to my hometown tonight. Despite my sombre mood, she holds my hands and offers words of courage to help me face the situation. She even suggests coming to my flat to provide comfort, but I humbly decline her generous act.

Walking alone towards my flat after parting ways with Kalyani, I find myself reflecting on my automatic decision not to invite her over. Despite her helpfulness, I still see her as somewhat distant, unlike a typical acquaintance.

Learning that my reluctance stems from an underlying concern for Kalyani's unfortunate circumstances, I acknowledge that this negative impression prevents me from inviting her into my home. Glancing back at her on the street, I watch as she climbs into an auto, her presence lingering in my thoughts as I continue on my solitary journey home.

The solitary train journey stirs up memories of all the moments I miss about travelling with Saira, especially our shared experiences on sleeper berths during bus journeys. As I sit by the window, my mind replays the blissful times we spent together on those berths, creating a nostalgic lens through which I view my surroundings.

Despite my attempt to focus on the passing scenery outside, I cannot help but notice a young couple engaged in affectionate gestures on an upper berth diagonally across from me. Respecting their privacy, I refrain from turning towards them and instead divert my attention to the city lights shimmering outside the window. Sleep eludes me, so I recline into a contemplative posture, gazing out at the world passing by.

The sight of towering apartments and gleaming glass office buildings captivates me, providing a welcome distraction from thoughts of our shared adventures on sleeper berths. Meanwhile, in the recesses of my mind, a stream of poetic lines begins to form—words that I contemplate including in an email to her.

As I embark on this day-long journey, an intriguing idea takes root in my mind and resonates with me throughout the entire train ride. I reflect on the six years we spent together, where Saira was completely herself without any inhibitions, cherishing every moment—including our disagreements. The intimacy we shared, the personal space we inhabited together, remains etched in my memory and heart, intertwined with our souls.

When I ponder the intricacies of our passionate connection, I am struck by a strong conviction that she could never allow anyone else into that sacred realm we cultivated together. Our shared experiences are like imprints on our bodies, sealed within our entwined hearts, and unify our souls as one. How then could I believe that she has forgotten me and has moved on completely? Surely, she must be thinking of me wherever she is.

This newfound sense of hope motivates me to consider reaching out to her on her upcoming birthday.

Fatigued from nearly a day of travel, I now find myself walking along the red, muddy path leading towards my village. I disembarked at Visakhapatnam station an hour ago and took a bus for the remaining 30 kilometres to my village. As I enter the main street of the village, the familiar scent of cattle waste and dry grass fills the air—a characteristic aroma that permeates rural life.

The brief ten-minute walk to my home is accompanied by the sight of neighbours returning their cattle from the grazing fields and motorcyclists carrying bundles of grass on their bikes. The setting sun signals the end of the day's activities, as the village usually settles into an early slumber by 8 or 9 o'clock.

Upon arriving at the familiar old compound wall, standing at a modest five feet tall with no gate, I feel a sense of warmth and motherly love wash over me even before I enter. It's a habit to clean my legs and hands before stepping inside the house, a routine ingrained from childhood.

Casually surveying the front yard, I notice the buffalo peacefully grazing. Usually, I would find my mother just outside the compound wall, but today she's nowhere in sight. She must be too weak to venture outside on her own.

As I step into the house, I'm met with the sight of my mother lying on a cot in the hall. Upon seeing me, she attempts to sit up, but I rush to her side, gently urging her to stay still. Sitting beside her on the cot, I take her hand in mine, and at that moment, my eyes well up with tears.

The neighbouring uncle then informs me about what transpired at the hospital, providing me with much-needed context and clarity about my mother's condition.

"She is fine now, but the doctor has suggested she consult a cardiologist this week. He visits our nearby town this Saturday," the uncle reports to me.

"I will definitely take her there," I assure him.

"There seems to be some issue in the ECG report," he adds.

Peering at the ECG results, though I lack the expertise to interpret them, I address my mother directly, "Mom, you need to eat well and rest adequately. Don't worry about work at home. I will manage everything with the help of Dasu."

Dasu is a labourer who assists with our farm work. Alongside a few other helpers, he aids my mother in managing our three-acre plot of land and tending to the cattle. Despite my earlier suggestion that she come and stay with me in the city, she prefers to remain at home, citing her attachment to the place. She often reminisces about how she and my father built this home during their younger years, when they worked in agriculture.

It has been three days since I returned home, and each day my mother's health has been improving. Last night, I heard her whispering in her sleep, but I couldn't make out what she was saying. When I woke up this morning at 7 o'clock, I couldn't find her anywhere in the house or the compound. I suspect she must have gone to tend the agricultural field despite my earlier instructions.

I begin to prepare myself to go and reprimand her for not taking her health seriously. The nights here in the village are less turbulent compared to those in the city, perhaps due to the change of surroundings and the associated memories.

Saira hasn't troubled my sleep lately, but she remains a constant presence in my dreams. It's strange; during our six years together, I never dreamt of her, but since our separation, she has haunted my subconscious. My entire being feels like an intoxicated haze, suffocating and impenetrable, trapping me in a whirlwind of memories and emotions.

I had hoped that visiting my native place would help alleviate the weight of our shared past, and initially, it did. However, the aura of our past togetherness gradually overwhelms the rustic simplicity of the village. It's like the bright sun emerging after days of thunderous rain in the monsoon—the sun triumphs, and so does she.

I approach my mother near the paddy fields beyond our village, feeling a mix of concern and frustration.

"Do you know about your condition? Why have you come to the fields today?" I raise my voice, trying to convey my worry.

My mother glances at me, her expression calm despite my agitation. "Have you had your breakfast? There's rice and curd in the kitchen. Have you eaten?"

I try to redirect the conversation back to her health. "Don't change the subject. I'm talking about your health. Didn't I tell you not to work until you've seen the cardiologist? We have an appointment tomorrow. You need to be cautious until then."

My frustration mounts as I notice her struggling to speak and gasping for breath while walking. "I thought I would be back before you woke up. The rain over the past two days has filled the nearby water bodies. It's the perfect time for sowing," she explains, attempting to justify her actions.

"Don't try to convince me, Mother! You are not going to the fields again this week. And remember— we are seeing the doctor tomorrow," I assert firmly, determined to prioritise her health and well-being over agricultural tasks.

******

As I sit in the waiting lounge at the scan centre near the hospital, one day before Saira's birthday, a sense of unease washes over me. My mother had disclosed multiple health issues to a compassionate doctor in a nearby town—chronic neck pain that had worsened recently, and problems with her lower back. She was taken into the MRI scan room about ten minutes ago, and I am left waiting outside.

Based on her symptoms, the doctor recommended scans of her brain and spine, a process that will take nearly twenty minutes. The discovery of these new health concerns has left me feeling disheartened, and I long for someone to be by my side during this trying time. I find myself hoping for a call from a friend, someone to check in and offer support. Yet, I acknowledge that my own actions have led to my current loneliness.

Reflecting on my past, I regret severing ties with my old friends while I was with her. I often avoided meeting them and sometimes even ignored their calls, causing them to gradually drift away from me. I didn't fully grasp the impact of losing those connections until after she left me. In hindsight, I deeply regret my choices.

As the rhythmic beeping of the scan machine fills the sterile air around me, I find myself lost in introspection, grappling with the weight of my mother's health concerns. Suddenly, the jarring ringtone of my phone pierces through my reverie, pulling me back to the present moment. It's Kalyani on the line, her voice a comforting anchor in the sea of my worries.

"Hello, how is your mother doing?" Kalyani's genuine concern echoes through the phone, instantly easing my heartache. Her warmth extends beyond mere pleasantries as she effortlessly transitions into light-hearted banter, bringing a sense of levity to our conversation.

"You don't need to worry, my friend! You are truly one of a kind," Kalyani reassures me, her words like a balm to my troubled soul. "Since I met you that night, you've been on my mind constantly. It's the first time I've thought about someone so much. Pure hearts like yours may face trials, but they will ultimately find peace."

Her compassionate sentiments resonate deeply within me, stirring a sense of validation and hope that I've sorely missed. For the first time in a while, the self-doubt and negative self-image that have plagued me begin to dissipate.

Encouraged by Kalyani's unwavering support, I feel inspired to compose a heartfelt email for her upcoming birthday. With renewed clarity and purpose, I reach for my phone and start typing. The words flow effortlessly from my fingertips, guided by a newfound sense of connection and gratitude.

In those moments of writing, I am no longer just penning words on a screen; I am weaving together emotions and aspirations, expressing truths that have long been tucked away in the recesses of my heart. With each keystroke, I feel a weight lift from my shoulders, replaced by a quiet resolve to embrace life's challenges with courage and resilience.

As I read over the completed message in my notes, a sense of contentment washes over me. This isn't merely an email; it's a testament to the profound impact of human connection and the transformative power of genuine empathy.

"May your sparkling eyes
Always light up cheers around,
Let your chaste smile
Never cease to steal the hearts,
May your mellifluous tone
Pull my soul out of lethargy,
Let your presence in my heart
Lead me as a beacon in times of darkness;
May your indomitable spirit
Perch you on the pinnacle of success,
Let the true self of yours
Be endlessly worshipped in my heart.
Happy birthday, my LOVE!"

As I read the birthday note I've composed for Saira meticulously, the vivid image of her at the end of the corridor begins to play tricks on my mind. Despite the intensity of my longing, I remain grounded in reality, acknowledging that she is not truly there. The distinction between reality and illusion remains palpable in my senses.

Meanwhile, my mother emerges from the doctor's room, her presence a welcome distraction from my wistful thoughts. I accompany her as we head to consult with the doctor regarding her health concerns.

Later that evening, in the quietude of our home, I focus on crafting a special birthday note for Saira. With care, I paste her photograph beside the heartfelt lines I've already typed. My mother, weary from the day's hospital visits, rests in her bedroom after a light meal.

Unfortunately, we were unable to meet the doctor to discuss the test results due to an emergency case. However, we have the results in hand and are scheduled to meet him the following day to gain further insights into my mother's health condition.

The anticipated night has arrived, and the clock reads 11:30 PM. Despite the late hour, sleep eludes me as I periodically check on my mother resting in the adjacent room. In tandem, I precisely draft the email destined for Saira, set to be sent precisely at midnight. With everything prepared, I await the opportune moment to hit send.

Even within the confines of my home, my thoughts are consumed by Saira, imagining how she might be feeling and perhaps missing me at this significant hour. As the minutes tick closer to midnight, a surge of determination builds within me, reinforcing my resolve to definitively send the email.

I hear a sudden sound from my mother's room, like a steel glass falling from the small wooden stool beside her bed. Alarmed, I rush to her side and find her gasping and struggling to breathe. She appears disoriented and unable to respond to my calls.

Frantically, I try to comfort her and call out to her repeatedly, but she remains unresponsive, lost in her own distress. Tears well up in my eyes as I feel helpless at this moment of urgency. Gently placing her back on the cot, I dash to my uncle's house nearby and urgently wake him.

My uncle arrives promptly, assessing the situation and determining that we must take her to a local clinic immediately. We have decided to transport her to a nearby RMP (Registered Medical Practitioner) in the next village for urgent medical attention.

As we speed towards the hospital in the auto-rickshaw, I sit in the backseat with my mother resting on my lap. I gently stroke her head, attempting to offer some comfort in the unsettling journey. My uncle, seated beside the driver, keeps a watchful eye on my mother's condition, turning back frequently to check on her.

The biting cold wind cuts through us, making it particularly harsh for my mother. Thankfully, I had brought a blanket along to shield her from the chill. I wrap my left arm around her, reassuring her to stay awake as we approach the hospital. However, I'm unsure if my voice is reaching her in her distressed state.

Despite the urgency of the situation, my mind is divided. While I focus on my mother's well-being and the dark road ahead, my thoughts stray to Saira. I find myself intermittently checking my phone, anxiously awaiting the opportune moment to send her the birthday email. My heart remains fixated on being the first to wish her on her special day, despite the turbulence of the present moment.

As my uncle ascends the staircase to wake the doctor, I stand at the entrance of the clinic section on the ground floor, holding my mother wrapped in a blanket with my arm around her. I find some solace in feeling her breathing against me, a familiar comfort surrounded by the turmoil.

My uncle's persistent knocks on the door finally yield a response, and the doctor appears. With my mother still in my arms, we are led into the clinic area. The doctor begins to explain my mother's condition, but my mind is too clouded to fully comprehend his words. I gather that he intends to administer saline and medication intravenously.

Carefully, I help my mother lie down on a raised wooden bench as the doctor prepares for the treatment. As I glance at my mobile screen, the time reads 11:58. The urgency to send the birthday email to Saira weighs heavily on my mind, juxtaposed against the immediate concern for my mother's health.

As the doctor administers the I.V. drip and prepares injections, I open the Gmail app and navigate to my draft email. With my mother receiving medical attention, I type in her email address and set the subject as "Happy Birthday, My Love!".

In perfect synchronisation, I hit the send button just as the doctor finishes the procedure. Yet, even as I watch the email dispatch, a pang of uncertainty grips me. Will she ever see my message? Uncertain of her response, I open WhatsApp, determined to reach her directly. I attach the same photo and type out a heartfelt birthday message. With a deep breath, I hit send, only to notice a single tick on the message, an indication that she may have already blocked me.

The revelation hits hard, mingling with the concern for my mother's well-being. Standing there in the clinic, enveloped in the sterile environment and the hum of medical activity, I feel a profound mix of emotions—hope, despair, and the recurring ache of unanswered questions about Saira.

Chapter 5: The Winding Path

Standing on the bustling main road, my backpack perches lightly on my right shoulder, holding just the essentials for a journey into the unknown. Its contents—a change of clothes and necessities—seem trivial compared to the weight of intangible burdens I carry: memories that cling like shadows, emotions that tug at my heart, expectations that flicker with diminishing hope, and the lingering ache of loss. As I gaze down the road, uncertainty stretches ahead like an uncharted path, mirroring the ambiguity of my current destination.

Clad in attire that neither suggests an interview nor a romantic escapade, I am an enigma to passersby, a traveller without a clear purpose. My mother, whose health has remarkably improved over the past week, prompted this spontaneous journey. Her suggestion of a solo expedition into nature and new experiences was offered with the wisdom of someone who has weathered life's storms. Though her rationale remains a mystery to me, I trust her insights, knowing she sees beneath the surface of my calm facade.

Since the night my mother was hospitalised, I believed I had been attentive to her needs, protecting her from the weight of my own burdens. Unbeknownst to me, she observed the turmoil etched in my expressions, perhaps sensing the depth of my inner struggles. Despite her perceptive nature, she chose silence over probing questions, allowing me space to navigate my emotions.

As I stand at this crossroads, my thoughts drift between the past and the uncertain future, mingling with the hum of passing traffic. The road ahead beckons with promises of discovery, a journey that mirrors the quest to reconcile my inner turmoil and rediscover a sense of purpose.

"Oh my heavens! Look who's there!" The exclamation cuts through my wandering thoughts, drawing my attention to the source of the loud shout. It takes a moment for me to fully emerge from my thoughts and focus on the scene unfolding before me.

"Hey, Saint! What a great surprise to find you here!" Kalyani's enthusiastic wave beckons me over from the other side of the road. She's behind the wheel of an old Jeep, which she's parked nearby. Intrigued and slightly taken aback by the unexpected encounter, I walk toward her, my curiosity piqued and a smile tugging at the corners of my lips.

"What brought you here? This is quite a shock!" I call out as I approach the driver's side, eager to understand the reason behind her sudden appearance.

"Get into the Beast first," she playfully invites me with a mischievous grin. "I mean the Jeep, boy! I've named it 'the Beast' because it's perfect for exploring mountains and jungles, and that's exactly where we're headed on this adventure." As I climb into the vehicle, I'm struck by the contrast between the weathered exterior and the surprisingly tidy interior. Kalyani greets me warmly, running her right palm through my hair affectionately, a gesture that catches me off guard but fills me with a sense of comfort.

"Where did you find this amazing Beast? The interiors are impressive despite its rough exterior," I remark, still slightly puzzled yet genuinely intrigued by the unexpected encounter and the unconventional vehicle.

"Quite remarkable, isn't it? One should be clean on the inside regardless of appearances," she replies cryptically, her words carrying a deeper meaning that I can't fully decipher at the moment.

"What are you saying? Where are we heading?" I press for answers, unable to contain my curiosity about Kalyani's sudden appearance and her cryptic comments.

"I was planning to make a call after reaching your village, but luckily, I stumbled upon you here on the main road. By the way, where are you off to? Is your mom doing well?" Kalyani inquires, her concern evident in her voice and demeanour.

"Yeah, she's feeling better now," I reply with a hint of relief. "Seeing me in such a state, she suggested I take a trip into nature to clear my mind and find some peace."

"It's true. I'm on a journey of sorts myself. I actually wanted to visit you when you were at the hospital with your mother, but circumstances got in the way. Whenever I think of you enduring such pain, my heart aches. Most people wouldn't survive such heartbreak, but you're someone special," Kalyani empathises with my struggles.

"When did you come to this region?" I ask Kalyani, my mind still grappling with the recent tumultuous events.

"Just yesterday," Kalyani responds with a thoughtful expression. "I wanted to see you right away, but I figured you might be busy taking care of your mom. Luckily, I have a friend here who helped me get this Beast. I named it, of course, and set out this morning intending to bring you along."

"I already feel like this trip is much needed. Is there anyone else joining us?" I inquire, a spark of excitement igniting within me.

"Yes, about fifteen kilometres from here, another saint will be joining us," Kalyani replies with a mysterious smile.

"Wow! That's great! I look forward to meeting our new companion," I respond, feeling a sense of camaraderie and anticipation.

"You must meet him. He shares the same purity of soul as you," Kalyani remarks warmly, using the endearing term that never fails to lift my spirits.

As we continue along the winding road, enveloped by lush greenery and picturesque arch-like formations, memories of Saira begin to surface once again. The beauty of the landscape contrasts sharply with the emotional turmoil within me.

On Saira's birthday night, since I took a leap of faith by reaching out via email, followed by a hopeful message on WhatsApp, the absence of a response gnawed at my soul. I found myself ensnared in a cycle of checking and rechecking my inbox, clinging to the screen of my phone like a lifeline in turbulent waters, desperate for a connection that remained elusive. Then, unexpectedly, I stumbled upon a WhatsApp status posted by Saira's friend, Madhuri. It was a video clip featuring Saira, joyfully singing and dancing on a city street, encircled by friends, clearly celebrating her birthday.

"Today is my birthday... It's my birthday today..." Her voice echoed in the video, accompanied by cheers and applause from her friends. Despite the happiness radiating from Saira in the clip, a wave of bittersweet emotion washed over me, leaving my eyes moist with unspoken longing.

Seeing Saira so vibrant and carefree after nearly a year apart filled me with conflicting emotions. Part of me was thrilled to catch a glimpse of her happiness, but another part couldn't shake the painful realisation that she seemed to have moved on without a second thought. The undeniable truth hit me like a tidal wave—I had been left behind.

As we traverse this scenic route, I can't help but reflect on the profound question that plagues my mind: *"Have I become so insignificant and undeserving in her eyes?"* Despite my inner turmoil, one question continues to evade an answer: *"Why can't I harbor any bitterness or animosity toward Saira, even after everything?"* It's a mystery I doubt I'll ever unravel on my own, perhaps requiring an outsider's perspective to shed light on the crux of my emotional struggle. Deep down, I know the problem lies within me, but finding a solution remains an elusive quest.

Lost in my thoughts, I'm jolted back to the present by Kalyani's voice, calling out to me amid the tranquil woodland background. The Jeep comes to a gentle halt at a narrow crossroad, and I turn to Kalyani with eager anticipation, wondering what surprise awaits us next. Her eyes sparkle in response to mine, suggesting that something intriguing lies ahead.

"Don't you want to meet the other saint?" Kalyani teases playfully, her voice filled with anticipation.

"Of course, I do! Where is he?" I scan the place, trying to discern the next part of our adventure. Kalyani motions for us to disembark, indicating that we need to walk a short distance from here to our destination.

We ascend along an upward road that winds toward a high cliff, offering glimpses of a bridge-like structure in the distance. To the left, a vast park sprawls beneath the road, while to the right, a towering hillside looms, adding a dramatic backdrop to our surroundings.

"It's the reservoir," I exclaim with a touch of nostalgia, memories from childhood flooding back at the sight.

"Yes, indeed. Have you been here recently?" Kalyani inquires, her gaze sweeping over the landscape with appreciation.

"Not in recent years. I remember coming here on a school excursion during childhood. We were allowed to explore the gardens down there," I recall, my mind drifting back to simpler times filled with youthful wonder.

As we continue our ascent, we arrive at the entrance gate of the bridge leading to the expansive water gates. The landscape unfolds before us like a painting—a breathtaking panorama of hills encircling a central water body, with the road we stand on skirting the bund beside the reservoir.

"Sometimes, we fail to appreciate the beauty of nature that beckons us from nearby," Kalyani remarks thoughtfully, her words resonating with the scene before us. "We're always dreaming of far-off and exotic destinations, but we overlook the wonders right in front of us."

I am left speechless as the vista captivates my senses—a mesmerising display of nature's grandeur. The water glistens under the sunlight, inviting us closer, but the gate obstructs our path. Undeterred, Kalyani veers off onto a side path beyond the boundary wall, and with a surge of excitement, I follow suit. My legs move instinctively, propelled by the allure of this natural paradise unfolding before me, each step revealing more of the hidden beauty tucked away in this familiar yet often overlooked ambience.

The serene reservoir, nestled between encroaching hills, presents a tranquil scene that captivates my senses. Its surface, like a mirror, reflects the details of the expansive sky above—a captivating display of nature's beauty. The morning light adds a touch of extravagance, painting the scene with vibrant colours that enhance the overall sense of tranquillity. I find myself drawn to the soothing clarity of the water, which seems untouched by the chaos of the world beyond.

As we continue our stroll, we reach a closed stair post, fenced off by iron grills. Kalyani, though not familiar with these regions, effortlessly vaults over the gate, encouraging me to follow suit. Descending the steps, I notice a solitary figure seated by the water's edge—a man with short, spiky hair showcasing a striking blend of black and gray. He is engrossed in the act of fishing, his patient demeanour adding to the atmosphere of calm solitude that pervades the area.

"Meet Vishwa, the other saint," Kalyani announces with a playful flourish, gesturing towards the man by the water. Vishwa turns to greet us, his face bearing traces of beedi smoke, a testament to his relaxed disposition. He extends a hand in greeting, a humble acknowledgement of our presence.

"This is indeed a remarkable day—a meeting of two 'saints' in this paradise," Kalyani remarks with a mischievous grin, underscoring the unique encounter and the natural beauty of the reservoir. Her infectious enthusiasm infuses the moment with a sense of playful camaraderie, setting the tone for our interaction with Vishwa.

"Any luck with the fish?" Kalyani inquires, striking up a conversation with Vishwa as we approach. Meanwhile, my attention is drawn to a sign affixed to the nearby wall— 'Fishing or swimming is prohibited here!'—a curious juxtaposition against the intimate background.

Vishwa, observing my curiosity, offers a wry comment, "This area is restricted. That's why you find forbidden things happening here." His eyes hint at a hidden world beyond the mundane, a realm where secret activities unfold around the reservoir.

Intrigued by Vishwa's cryptic behaviour, we follow him towards a dense cluster of bushes, where he deftly pushes aside vines to reveal a hidden scene. Peering through the foliage, we are astonished to witness a young couple—lost in their private world—engaged in tender moments by the water's edge. The boy's persistent attempts to escalate their intimacy are met with playful resistance from the girl, who maintains a shy hesitation.

As the atmosphere shifts, the boy's affections gradually soften the girl's resolve, and she eventually acquiesces to his desires. Suddenly, the boy produces a mobile phone, placing it strategically on a nearby rock to capture their intimate encounter—a voyeuristic twist that adds an unexpected layer to the scene.

Kalyani immediately rushes to the bush by shouting. "Hey, who is over there? Come out at once, or I'll call the police." Kalyani's sudden outburst startles the young man, who quickly flees, leaving the girl half-naked and distraught on the rocky bank. She struggles to compose herself as we approach, tears streaming down her face in embarrassment and fear.

"Stop crying! Nothing bad has happened," Vishwa shouts at her.

Kalyani, pushing Vishwa aside, enters with a fiery glare aimed at the girl. "In fact, you should be grateful for escaping something that would inevitably bring ruin upon you and your family. Never trust someone who lures you with temporary pleasures," she warns sternly. "I urge you to cut ties with him immediately, or else one day your intimate video will find its way onto adult websites and spread like wildfire across social media platforms. Don't sacrifice your family for momentary satisfaction. Now, leave this place," Kalyani commands, her words instilling fear in the girl, who climbs the rocks, tears streaming down her face, to reach the road.

Vishwa, still simmering with anger, expresses regret for not intervening sooner. "I would have dealt with that boy myself," he mutters, his frustration palpable. Kalyani's response is sharp and uncompromising, reflecting her zero-tolerance stance towards exploitation and deceit.

"How can you be so sure he lured her?" I interject, my curiosity piqued by Kalyani's decisive actions.

"Her reactions were telling—her shyness and tears. A girl truly in love wouldn't react that way," Kalyani explains, her tone tinged with empathy for the girl's predicament.

Back in the Jeep, Kalyani lights a cigarette, a moment of relaxation from the intensity of the recent events. Vishwa's inquiry about her sudden fervour prompts a reflective response from Kalyani, her eyes distant and reflective.

"Some memories last forever, especially those tied to physical encounters," Kalyani reflects, acknowledging the lasting impact of traumatic experiences.

The brief silence that follows is filled with unspoken contemplation, each of us lost in our thoughts and memories, navigating the emotional aftermath of the encounter.

Kalyani breaks the silence, shifting her focus back to the journey ahead. With purposeful resolve, she starts the engine, her gaze fixed on the road ahead.

"Where to now?" she asks Vishwa, her tone more composed but still carrying an air of determination.

"To Tulasi's Home," Vishwa replies. Kalyani's silence hints at a deeper significance, setting the stage for the next chapter of our journey.

As the Beast carries us forward along the winding road, enveloped by the tunnel-like canopy of trees, the dappled sunlight filtering through the foliage creates a mesmerising play of light and shadow on the path. Each fleeting beam illuminates patches of the road, highlighting the encompassing greenery and lending an ethereal quality to our ambience. The vista opens up to our side—a sweeping valley veiled in mist, framed by towering peaks that seem to embrace the horizon. Below, a cluster of cottages dots the landscape, imbuing the scene with a sense of remote tranquillity and timeless beauty. The cool mountain breeze carries with it a whisper of solitude, prompting contemplation and evoking a yearning for deeper connections.

The Beast comes to a gentle stop at a roadside viewpoint, where we are treated to a breathtaking panorama of the valley below. Beside us, a cascade of water descends from the cliff, its journey continuing beneath the road, adding a soothing soundtrack to the majestic vista. Peering over the edge, I catch a glimpse of the distant waterfall, its powerful descent contrasting with the serene backdrop of the valley floor. From this elevated vantage point, the merging of cascading water and lush greenery unfolds like a painting, captivating our senses and inviting us to pause and appreciate nature's grandeur.

The tranquil melody of trickling water harmonises with the distant roar of the waterfall, creating a symphony that reverberates through the canyon. Above us, unfamiliar trees sway in the breeze, their verdant foliage providing shelter from the drizzle. Intrigued by the diverse flora enfolding us, I observe as Vishwa and Kalyani deftly arrange our impromptu picnic. They lay out mats and unpack an assortment of snacks, presenting a delightful array of flavours on small paper plates. We gather around this makeshift feast, each selecting from the spread and relishing the blend of spicy and sweet treats in the setting of nature's symphony.

This immersion in nature feels wholly transformative—an experience that transcends the ordinary constraints of time and obligation. Covered by pristine wilderness and the harmonious sounds of the natural world, I am struck by the liberating absence of time's grip. Here, in the company of newfound companions, we revel in the present moment, unhindered by the pressures of schedules and deadlines.

The brief respite in nature feels profoundly transformative, even within the span of a few moments. None of us suggests leaving; instead, we extend our stay, allowing ourselves to be fully immersed in the moment. As we share some snacks and a smoke, a sense of genuine happiness washes over me—a sensation I haven't felt in quite some time. Nature and the company of Kalyani and Vishwa seem to be slowly eroding the sharp edges of painful memories, replacing them with a newfound sense of peace and contentment. The shared smoking session feels like an unspoken therapy, offering insights into how to break free from the tangled web of past reminiscences.

"Transcending time is the greatest pursuit one can undertake," I muse inwardly, addressing myself. *"To find solace in the timeless embrace of nature and kindred spirits—is this not the essence of true liberation?"* My reverence hovers in the air, resonating with the profound impact of our journey and the potential for deeper introspection amid nature's timeless expanse. Each breath of mountain air, each rustle of leaves, seems to echo with unspoken truths waiting to be discovered in the stillness of the mountainside.

"Beholding such beauty imposes many constraints, doesn't it? One must shed those constraints to truly connect with nature's inspiration," Vishwa muses, his voice taking on a contemplative tone. Kalyani, fixated on the cascading water, appears lost in thought, her gaze tracing the path of the waterfall from its celestial origin down to earth. Gradually, I begin to grasp the depth of Vishwa's observation. During my trips with Saira near Bengaluru, though shrouded by breathtaking scenery, my focus was always drawn back to her beauty. Now, separated from her, I find myself fully present in nature, relishing the profound connection it offers—a communion not dictated by physical proximity, but by the freedom to embrace divinity within.

"Some are tethered to their companions, others absorbed in capturing photos on their mobiles, missing their true reflection in nature's mirror, while some are burdened by thoughts of tomorrow's tasks," Vishwa continues, gesturing to the enchanting canopy that has become our sanctuary. I interject, feeling compelled to add another layer to his observation. Both Vishwa and Kalyani turn towards me, their expressions urging me to elaborate.

"Indeed, there are those ensnared by the past," I admit, my voice tinged with introspection. "I'm not certain if I've entirely broken free, but I'm striving to discern the difference." The words reverberate in the air, mingling with the rustle of leaves and the distant rush of water, each syllable echoing the ongoing journey of self-discovery into nature's timeless embrace.

"No wonder I call you saints!" Kalyani suddenly breaks the silence, addressing Vishwa and me, after being captivated by the place until now. Our introduction at the reservoir hadn't led to much conversation between us. As she reveals our commonality, a welcoming smile spreads across both our faces, concealing the depths of our shared emotional turmoil. I knew little about Vishwa, and from his expression, he seemed equally curious about me.

"There's a common element in both of you. Each of you has loved a girl sincerely and is still living with her even after she left," Kalyani continues, her words resonating with our shared sense of longing and loss.

A monologue begins in my mind, echoing with newfound hope. *"I thought I was the only one afflicted with this unending ache. I've been desperately seeking a way to break free from her grip, but it feels impossible. And now, here I am, encountering someone else in the same relentless pursuit. Perhaps by understanding his journey, I might uncover my path to redemption."*

"Both of you are in a penance of love that essentially lasts forever. The divinity in you continues even though you don't communicate with them directly," Kalyani elaborates, capturing the essence of our enduring connection to lost love.

"No," I interject, compelled to share my own experience. "I have tried to reach out to her." Kalyani and Vishwa lean in, their eyes attentive as I recount my recent attempts. "I sent her emails and WhatsApp messages on her birthday just a week ago. Most of the time, I suppress the urge to contact her, but sometimes the weight of my emotions spills into a message. Yet, I received no response, and I don't even know if she read my messages."

"How does it feel when she ignores you like that?" Kalyani inquires, her posture reflecting genuine interest as she rests her chin on both palms, resembling a contemplative plant perched on a rock.

"I can't bear it when she disregards me," I confess, the pain of rejection evident in my voice. "Countless times, I've checked those apps, hoping for any sign that she acknowledges my existence. Then, the next day, I stumbled upon a video clip of her enjoying her birthday with friends at midnight, shared as a WhatsApp status. It tore me apart instantly. While she appeared joyful, I remained entangled in her web."

"And she hasn't responded until now?" Kalyani's question hangs in the air, highlighting the unending silence that echoes the depths of my unresolved emotions.

"No. With my mother in the hospital, my duty was to attend to her wholeheartedly. However, my attention often strayed from her due to thoughts of Saira. It's a shame on my part, I know. I feel like I haven't been a good son or a good person. But what can

I do? Giving up on her is not something I can do. The next day after her birthday, I sent her another email since she had already blocked me on WhatsApp. It was a poetic piece inspired by her beautiful picture that I saw on my mobile. Then I sent another email the following day. This routine continued until yesterday. I wrote her a new poem every day and sent it to her. A week of consecutive sleepless nights worried my mother. She understood that I was in deep trouble, which is why she urged me to leave and go back to work, in the hope that it would bring me some solace. Yet here we are, still talking about her, and I find her in every element of nature around me."

"Do you want to continue sending her emails or messages?" Vishwa inquires gently.

"My heart yearns to reach out to her again. On the other hand, I understand her last message when she said she had moved on in life. I believe she must be waiting for my messages, even though she has every right to remain silent and keep me at bay. Still, every cell in my body and soul longs to write to her despite her indifference."

"Why did she leave you in the first place?" Vishwa's question catches me off guard, and it takes me a moment to compose myself.

"It was…" I begin, but Kalyani interrupts gently, sensing my distress.

"No need to delve into that painful part, especially for a true lover. Reliving those moments of departure countless times is heart-wrenching enough. It doesn't matter why they broke up," she adds, turning to Vishwa. "The reason pales in comparison to the anguish of the breakup. Everything ends eventually, and this, too, has ended. That is the ultimate truth. Everything else is a myth, a trance, some kind of mirage in life. What matters now is how to accept it and move forward."

Her words resonate deeply, reminding me of the imperative to embrace the present and look towards the future, letting go of the haunting shadows of the past.

"What have you done for me?" The inevitable response reverberating in my mind surges out. "It's this kind of thinking that initiates the end. That's all I can trace." This must be the culmination of relentless analysis that has been occupying my thoughts for months.

Silence falls upon us for a few minutes, interrupted only by the cool breeze and the rhythm of tiny waves splashing against stones along the stream's edge. The lively chirping of birds and insects adds to the atmosphere, enhancing the contemplative mood.

"But why can't I let her go like that?" I continue to vent, feeling a weight lifted off my chest by sharing my thoughts. "Why can't I forget even the smallest details of our relationship? Look! As I speak with you now, I see that hedge over there, and my mind's eye serves as a screen replaying moments spent with her on a similar landscape during one of our trips. Will it ever stop?"

"It doesn't stop until you make it happen. Love might come naturally, but it never ceases by itself. You need a strong will to intentionally move past it." Vishwa makes a stern remark.

"What do you mean?" I'm surprised to be discussing these matters with someone for the first time, finding solace in the unexpected empathy.

"What time is it?" Vishwa asks me, shifting the focus of our conversation.

I twist my wrist towards him, displaying the dial of my watch with its brown strap and round face. "Ten minutes past three. But why?"

"Who gifted you the watch?" He points out, directing my attention to a meaningful detail.

I stare at the watch, momentarily at a loss for words, the weight of its significance sinking in.

"It must have been her, right?" Vishwa suggests drawing a connection.

I nod in agreement, realising the watch is a tangible link to memories I struggle to release.

"You want to change everything around you but not the part of yourself that has long been intertwined with her, buddy! You don't really want to let her go. Otherwise, you would have left the watch at home or in Bengaluru. Every moment you feel her, and you love it, even though it's sheer suffering."

"It's not that I don't want to move on… truly, I don't know how to."

"Throw the watch in the water to prove that you genuinely want to let her go." Vishwa's suggestion is both daunting and liberating, challenging me to confront my attachment head-on.

I remain calm, unwilling to comply with Vishwa's demand to throw away the watch. Kalyani's repeated glances at the watch and my reluctance to part with it betray the depth of my attachment. Vishwa, assuming an authoritative stance, begins loading items into the Jeep, and I mechanically follow suit, lost in my thoughts. *'Despite my efforts over the months to distance myself from reminders of her—disconnecting from mutual friends, abandoning shared interests, and relocating—this watch has persisted as a silent companion, dictating every moment of my existence.'*

"What? It's still on your wrist? It means you don't want to let her go; you've merely lost her, which was never your intention," Vishwa concludes astutely.

"Please, let's just go from here!" I implore, slamming the door shut as I retreat to the back seat, unable to bear Vishwa's incisive discovery.

As the Beast resumes its journey, the sun shines brightly overhead, yet its rays struggle to pierce through the dense canopy of overhanging trees that line the road.

"Are we heading to Tulasi's home in Ananthagiri now?" Kalyani seeks confirmation from her position behind the wheel. The Beast continues its leisurely pace along the winding road, passing through verdant tunnels of greenery and encountering curious monkeys. The surroundings intermittently darken, resembling the onset of evening.

"Yes, that's our destination. I believe we'll arrive by evening," Vishwa affirms.

"Good, we don't need to rush," Kalyani responds.

"Who is Tulasi, and why are we going to her home?" I finally break my inner silence, curious about the purpose of our visit.

Kalyani looks at Vishwa, expecting him to provide an answer. However, he remains silent. After a minute, she takes it upon herself to reveal, "Tulasi is his love, the love of his life."

"Wow! It's intriguing to go and meet her now. What's your story? I'd love to hear it in full detail. Would you mind sharing it with me?" I direct my request to Vishwa, eager to understand the narrative.

"Certainly, I'd be happy to share, but perhaps our friend Kalyani would equally enjoy recounting it," Vishwa replies, passing the opportunity back to her.

"I don't have all the details of the story. It would be better if you tell it," Kalyani refers to Vishwa.

After a couple of silent minutes, Vishwa agrees to share his story. Meanwhile, I've prepared the content for my next email to Saira, and I'm attempting to open the Gmail app to send it. Despite multiple attempts, the app fails to load due to the lack of a network signal on my mobile. Vishwa notices my distress with the phone and offers reassurance, "We haven't reached Ananthagiri Hills yet. You'll get a signal there. Just have patience."

Feeling uncomfortable being caught in the act of composing messages to Saira, I promptly close the mobile and stow it away in my pocket.

"I was born into a middle-class, conventional family from a backward caste," Vishwa begins his narrative. "My father was a priest at the Hanuman temple in our village. You know, not all priests are Brahmins here. Some from other castes also learn the rituals and serve in temples. Occasionally, my father would ask for my help during special occasions, which I often avoided for no particular reason. One day during a festival, instead of assisting him, I wandered into the hilly areas and encountered Tulasi, a tribal girl."

He continues, "I followed Tulasi and discovered that she was heading towards the temple. I decided to join her there. Unfortunately, my father spotted me and insisted that I stay with him until the afternoon. This was the first time Tulasi noticed me, and I couldn't ignore my father's command. Throughout her brief visit to the temple, I made every effort to catch her gaze. Her beautiful smile enchanted me, transporting me to another world. Even after she left, I remained captivated by this new fantasy, performing my temple duties with a sense of distraction."

In the following week, my anticipation for Tulasi's visit to the temple on Saturday was filled with hope and eagerness. Each passing day brought a growing sense of excitement as I envisioned our potential encounter. As Saturday arrived, I positioned myself along the path leading to the temple, eagerly awaiting her arrival. However, as the day progressed and the temple rituals unfolded, it became apparent that Tulasi was not going to show up.

Determined to find her, I decided to venture in the opposite direction, exploring the hamlet where she lived. The village streets were quiet and serene, lined with modest thatched houses. After an hour of wandering, I finally spotted her in the front yard of a quaint house at the far end of a narrow street.

Tulasi's appearance that day was a stark contrast to how I had seen her at the temple. She was dressed in a traditional half saree, her hair neatly tied at the back of her head. The pallu of her saree was draped loosely, revealing her waistline and navel, adding an alluring touch to her rustic beauty. Her skirt, raised just below the knee, accentuated her allure amidst the simple rural setting.

When Tulasi caught a rooster, her eyes met mine, momentarily forgetting her task. In that fleeting moment, I felt a connection, and it seemed as if time stood still. However, her grandmother's shout quickly brought her back to reality, and she resumed her chores, stealing glances at me until I disappeared from view.

That night, I lay awake, unable to sleep, consumed by thoughts of Tulasi. I couldn't shake the image of her captivating smile and the way her eyes had locked with mine. It was then that I realised she was more than just a passing fancy—she was the love of my life, and I was determined to make her mine.

Over the next two months, Tulasi and I explored every nook and cranny of the neighbouring hills and hedges together. The trees seemed to sway in rhythm to our love songs, bearing witness to our tender moments. Though we exercised restraint out of respect for our families and traditions, our encounters were filled with the bliss of innocent and chaste affection beneath the watchful gaze of the hillsides.

As our relationship blossomed, it inevitably drew attention and gossip within the village. News of our union spread like wildfire, reaching not only my family but also Tulasi's. The revelation of our relationship sparked turmoil and disapproval, particularly from my father, who held a respected position as a priest in the village temple.

The day I couldn't find Tulasi at our usual meeting spot beyond the agricultural lands, my heart sank. I waited until evening, hoping to catch a glimpse of her, only to receive the devastating news that she had been married the previous night in a distant village. Despite my efforts to see her again, I failed to even cast a glance at her face in the following month.

"Stop here," Vishwa's outcry startles both of us. The Beast suddenly screeches to a halt on the road. Slowly, Kalyani brings it to the side of the road, and Vishwa gets off.

We follow him into a narrow trail uphill on the left. Progressing through a few plantations in silence, we enter an open and plain tract of land near the cliff. Strangely, there are *tulsi* plants scattered all around. To the left, a hamlet sits on a higher plane, while to the right stretches a picturesque valley that looks like something out of a distant, exotic land.

Vishwa continues his walk until he reaches the hedge on the boundary of the cliff and stands in front of something. As I approach, I see two tombs side by side. On the tomb where Vishwa stands, with closed eyes, the name "Tulasi " is written. Shock courses through me, and I turn to Kalyani, but she is already in a prayer stance.

I stand there, my mind reeling with the weight of this revelation. Tulasi, the love of Vishwa's life, now rests beneath this tranquil spot overlooking the valley. The *tulsi* plants surrounding us seem to echo the profound loss and enduring love that Vishwa carries in his heart. Kalyani's prayer seems to fill the air with solemnity and reverence. I join her silently, offering my own thoughts and prayers to the memory of Tulasi and the bond she shared with Vishwa.

Chapter 6: Guilt and Punishment

In the evening, the cold wind whips against us on the hillside, cutting through the air with an icy hostility. The garden of tulsi plants has kept us company for over an hour now, their presence adding a poignant backdrop to the sad tale of Tulasi's life.

"For the next six months, the real moron in me came out," Vishwa begins, his voice tinged with regret. "I searched many places secretly, but couldn't trace her. I was consumed by her relentless thoughts. People told me stories about her supposedly dumping me, but I found them hard to believe. When I learned about her secret marriage with a man from a remote village in another district, I wanted to fall at her feet and convince her to run away with me, leaving her husband behind. I was certain that she would choose me the moment she saw me, no matter the circumstances she was in. But her family and new life were like a mystery I couldn't solve, which made me go crazy."

"Crazy?" I interject, struck by the intensity of Vishwa's emotions.

Vishwa sighs deeply before continuing, "Yes, I... I lost control. I wanted to sever all physical and emotional ties to Tulasi. I turned to other women for comfort, engaging in physical relationships with many of them. But every time I was with someone new, it was

Tulasi's face that haunted me. The more I tried to erase her from my heart, the more her memory consumed me. Yet, I didn't stop my reckless behaviour. If you had seen me during that time, you would have called me a pervert."

"A pervert?" I express concern, grappling with the weight of Vishwa's revelations about his desperate attempts to rid himself of Tulasi's memory.

"I pursued every attractive woman I encountered," Vishwa confesses, his voice heavy with remorse. "I grabbed every opportunity to win them over, desiring consolation in fleeting physical connections. I lost count of the women I slept with during that period - it was forty-five in total. I spent nights in countless resorts from Vizag to Araku, and even in secluded gardens and bushes along the way. I became like an animal, a monster driven by my own inner turmoil."

Vishwa's confession leaves a heavy silence hanging in the air, the weight of his actions palpable in the twilight. The wind continues to howl around us, echoing the tumultuous emotions stirred by his story. I am left speechless, grappling with the profound impact of Vishwa's journey through grief and desperation, his attempt to bury his pain in a sea of physicality.

As we stand amidst the fading light, the realisation dawns that beneath Vishwa's detached exterior lies a tumultuous soul grappling with the consequences of lost love. The tulsi plants sway gently around us, their leaves whispering a silent prayer for healing and redemption.

I am left gaping at Vishwa with my mouth wide open as he continues to narrate his unbridled carnal adventures.

"But I never resorted to prostitution," Vishwa continues, his voice tinged with a mix of regret and remorse. "All the women and girls I slept with came to me willingly, desiring companionship. They had desires of their own, and I merely exploited them for my own needs. There was a time when I had two women and a young girl in adjacent hotel rooms in Araku. I shifted between them over two days and nights, driven by an insatiable physical craving. Yet, even in such indulgence, I couldn't escape the memory of Tulasi. My attempts to erase her from my mind were futile."

Unintentionally, I glance at Kalyani with a question mark on my face, silently pursuing understanding. "I know what you're thinking," she responds, addressing the unspoken question. "I called him a saint and compared him to you. Isn't that what's on your mind?" I remain silent in agreement, taken aback by the layers of complexity unfolding in Vishwa's story. Kalyani gestures for Vishwa to continue, acknowledging that there is more to be revealed.

"I was swept away by my amorous adventures for three months," Vishwa confesses, his voice heavy with the weight of his own actions. "Then, one day, it all came crashing down when I saw Tulasi in our village. She visited the temple with her husband and in-laws. I managed to hide from her, overwhelmed by conflicting emotions. On one hand, I was elated to see her happy and beautiful as a grown woman, and on the other hand, I was devastated because she was no longer mine. Later that evening, I learned that their family had come to settle in the village."

The Beast veers off the main road, guided by Vishwa's directions. Kalyani navigates the narrow concrete streets of a village with determination, while I struggle to find a network signal on my mobile, growing increasingly frustrated. Tucking my phone back into my pocket, I resign myself to the unfolding journey.

Vishwa falls silent, lost in contemplation, as Kalyani drives through the quiet residential streets. I sense that they are leading me toward something significant. After a series of turns through the narrow streets, the Beast comes to a stop near a massive tree on a wide street, surrounded by a stone ridge where people can sit. No one else is around at the moment, but Vishwa disembarks and settles on the ridge, his gaze fixed pensively on an abandoned house across the street.

"He sat here every day, waiting for her to come out and see him," Kalyani continues, weaving the narrative of Vishwa's unrelenting devotion. "Unable to control himself without seeing her, knowing she was inside this house, he spent entire days here. People came and went from the house, yet no one noticed him. On the third day, she finally cast a glance at the rustic, beastly-looking young man who had been yearning for just a moment of acknowledgement from the married woman inside. That glance shattered her composure, and she burst into tears. To avoid any suspicion, she hurried inside after that brief interaction. Vishwa stood there, anxious but rooted to the spot, knowing he shouldn't intrude further. He waited until evening, but she did not reappear. As darkness fell and her husband returned home, Vishwa too left for his own home."

"This routine continued for the next two days," Kalyani narrates, her voice filled with empathy. "Tulasi would catch sight of him through the windows and quickly shut them, avoiding further contact. Still, Vishwa persisted, faithfully waiting under the tree. To avoid arousing suspicion, he gathered local children whenever possible and engaged them in board games beneath the shade of the tree."

"Finally, one afternoon when the house was quiet, she came running to him," Kalyani continues, her words painting a vivid scene. "She pleaded with him to go away, her tormented soul seeking forgiveness. She confessed her marriage and vowed never to forsake her husband. Speechless, Vishwa stood as she retreated back inside, the door closing behind her. Despite this encounter, he continued his daily vigil under the tree, enduring rain, scorching sun, and indifferent glances."

"Vishwa soon learned that her husband was in the army and was home on vacation," Kalyani explains, her voice carrying the weight of Vishwa's unyielding hope. "He anticipated that she would reach out to him once her husband departed. So he persisted in waiting for her under the tree, regardless of the weather or the cold reception from onlookers.

The day of her husband's departure arrived, but Tulasi did not emerge from the house as Vishwa had hoped," Kalyani continues, her tone sombre. "Despite numerous opportunities, she remained inside. Vishwa, undeterred by disappointment, continued to see Tulasi as the young girl who had once yearned to embrace him during their initial meeting.

A week passed with no change, and Vishwa continued his relentless efforts. Finally, one evening, Tulasi approached Vishwa and instructed him to wait the next day at the plantation where they used to meet in the past. Vishwa felt overjoyed and returned home, eagerly anticipating their meeting.

The following day, Vishwa waited at the plantation for an hour until Tulasi finally arrived. She appeared worried about being seen by villagers from a nearby corner. Despite the constant interruptions from passersby, they managed to talk for a couple of minutes, hiding behind trees and hedges whenever someone approached.

Growing irritated by the disruptions, Vishwa pleaded with Tulasi for a more private meeting. Reluctant to encourage him in that direction yet unable to refuse outright, Tulasi agreed to meet him in their backyard later that night. She instructed Vishwa to approach their house from the backyard and wait in the darkness until after midnight, assuring him that she would join him once her mother-in-law was asleep."

Kalyani paused her narration and gestured towards Vishwa, who nodded in agreement, ready to continue the story.

As Vishwa recounts this pivotal moment, the scene comes alive with vivid details and charged emotions. "As planned, I quietly made my way to the backyard at the stroke of midnight, my anticipation building with each passing moment. The night air was cool and filled with the hushed whispers of the breeze. I found a secluded spot and waited, the minutes stretching into what felt like an eternity.

Finally, Tulasi emerged from the back door, bathed in moonlight. She wore a stunning white saree adorned with delicate jasmine flowers woven into her intricately braided hair. The intoxicating fragrance of jasmine enveloped her, adding to her ethereal charm. My heart skipped a beat at the sight of her.

Tulasi gestured for me to join her under the shelter of the back veranda. With a reassuring smile, she whispered that her mother-in-law was sound asleep and wouldn't stir due to her medication. Drawing closer, she cautioned me to keep our conversation to hushed tones, mindful of the silent night.

Our souls connected in that intimate space. As we whispered sweet nothings, the distance between us seemed to disappear. Our hands found each other, fingers intertwining in a tender embrace. I could feel the warmth of her presence, a magnetic pull drawing us closer. In the soft glow of the moonlight, I leaned in, unable to resist the allure of her proximity. Our bodies brushed against each other, heightening the intensity of our shared moment. Finally, in a surge of passion, I pressed a gentle kiss to her neck, a silent testament to our burgeoning love.

Despite the risk and the weight of our circumstances, Tulasi's response was a silent consent. In that fleeting moment, our hearts connected through whispered confessions and stolen intimacy. I was utterly captivated by the taste of her kiss, her warmth enveloping me in a haze of desire. Despite her attempts to resist, I found myself irresistibly drawn to her, unable to deny the pull of our shared longing. Dominated by our pent-up passions, we surrendered to each other's embrace. In those fleeting moments, we lost ourselves in the bliss of our passion, oblivious to the world around us."

Vishwa recalls the raw emotions of their union, the conflict between their longing and the moral boundaries they were breaking. The tears welling up in his eyes reflect the emotional turmoil of reliving this memory, clouded by the weight of consequence and regret.

"We surrendered to the moment, our bodies intertwined on the cool floor, oblivious to the passage of time," he concludes, his voice laden with sorrow. "In that intimate space, all concerns faded away—the ticking clock, the outside world, and the complexities of Tulasi's marital status dissolved in the intensity of our shared lust. We explored the depths of our connection, our hearts beating as one, intoxicated by the rush of newfound love. Hours melted into each other as we indulged in each other's touch, our bodies entwined in a dance of intimacy and longing. With each tender caress and whispered vow, we sought solace in each other's arms, a sanctuary from the constraints of reality.

As the night drew to a close and the first light of dawn peeked over the horizon, we reluctantly parted, our cores entangled in a web of forbidden passion. Though the morning heralded the return to our separate lives, the memory of that night lingered—a silent promise of love and desire shared in the secrecy of the veranda."

As Vishwa falls silent, the air is heavy with unspoken questions and regrets. Kalyani's voice breaks the silence, offering a gentle reassurance amid the emotional turbulence that prevails.

"It's difficult to dwell on the past," Kalyani reflects, her voice a soft anchor amidst the emotional storm. "Let's redirect our thoughts towards the beauty of the falls nearby."

With that, they leave behind the weight of their shared memories, setting their sights on the natural wonder of Ananthagiri Falls—a respite from the emotional turbulence that grips their hearts.

The scene at Ananthagiri Falls is nothing short of awe-inspiring. Vishwa, fully immersed in the cascading water, stands beneath the roaring falls, his silhouette framed by the misty spray. Kalyani and I, on the banks of the stream, take in the tranquil beauty that surrounds us. As Vishwa relishes his nature bath, the sound of the water crashing down creates a rhythmic symphony that resonates deep within. The setting sun casts a warm, golden glow over the landscape, enhancing the dramatic contrast between light and shadow.

Lost in the moment, I can't help but let my thoughts drift back to Tulasi and the unanswered questions about her fate. The memory of her tomb, seen earlier, flashes in my mind like a haunting spectre, prompting unsettling speculations about what might have transpired after her clandestine encounter with Vishwa. In rural communities like Tulasi's, where societal judgments are swift and often merciless, I recall grim news stories of women facing severe consequences for perceived transgressions. The weight of these imagined horrors adds a melancholic undertone to the otherwise serene atmosphere.

Meanwhile, Vishwa beckons us to follow as he navigates downstream, his steps sure-footed on the rugged terrain. We traverse the landscape, hopping across moss-covered boulders and wading through crystal-clear streams, drawn closer to the edge of another mountain where the water plummets into the valley below.

Arriving at the precipice, we're greeted by the breathtaking spectacle of the waterfall in full glory. The sheer force of the cascading water creates a mesmerizing display, as sunlight refracts through the spray, painting rainbows in the mist.

Standing on the edge, enveloped by the sights and sounds of nature's grandeur, I feel a profound sense of awe and insignificance. The timeless dance of water against rock serves as a poignant reminder of the transient nature of human worries in the vast expanse of the natural world.

As the day draws to a close and the last rays of sunlight fade behind the horizon, I find relief in the beauty that surrounds me, a fleeting escape from the weight of unanswered questions and the haunting echoes of the past.

Vishwa's serene demeanour as he meditates in the natural splendour of Ananthagiri Falls captures the essence of his deep connection with the environment.

Perched on a large rock, his posture reflects a profound sense of tranquillity and oneness with his surroundings. The rhythmic melody of the cascading stream serves as a perfect backdrop, enhancing the meditative experience.

As Kalyani and I enjoy the guava fruits tossed to us by Vishwa, we can't help but admire his affinity for integrating with nature rather than merely observing it. The fruits, plucked fresh from the surroundings, add to the immersive experience of being in this pristine wilderness.

For me, however, the tranquillity of the moment is punctuated by the absence of mobile signals, temporarily halting my routine of sending emails to Saira. The brief respite from digital connectivity allows me to fully appreciate the natural beauty around me, yet my thoughts involuntarily gravitate towards her, as if her presence echoes in every corner of this wilderness.

Kalyani's remark about Vishwa's approach resonates deeply. It's evident that Vishwa pursues not just to witness nature's grandeur but to embrace it as an integral part of his being. His meditative posture symbolizes a harmonious union with the environment, a testament to his reverence for the earth's natural rhythms.

As we continue to savor the guava fruits and bask in the enchanting surroundings of Ananthagiri Falls, I find myself drawn into a deeper contemplation, contemplating the significance of Vishwa's meditative communion with nature and its implications for my own journey of self-discovery and inner peace.

The atmosphere around Vishwa as he recounts this part of his story is heavy with emotion, a mixture of regret, sorrow, and perhaps a hint of guilt for the events that transpired. As the day winds down and darkness descends upon the village, Vishwa's narrative takes on a bleak tone, reflecting the gravity of the situation.

"I must recount this part myself, for the suffering it continues to inflict upon me is part of the eternal punishment I bear for the grave sins I committed, particularly against a pure spirit like Tulasi. The next morning, I awoke unusually late at 11 a.m. When I ventured outside, I discovered a commotion in the village. Seeking answers, I looked for my mother or father, but my house was empty. After washing my face, I hurried into the street to learn what had occurred.

On my way to the temple, I overheard the talk of an army man from our village who had been killed in a border attack the previous night. Anxious, I made my way to Tulasi's home, where I found a throng of villagers gathered. A police Jeep was parked outside the gate, and I learned from fellow villagers that the Circle Inspector had visited to confirm the news of Tulasi's husband's demise.

The tragic news spread rapidly—there had been an unprecedented attack at the Indo-Pak border that night, claiming the lives of three army personnel, including Tulasi's husband. I was at a loss for how to react. Desperate to see Tulasi, I made repeated attempts to approach the compound, hoping for even a brief glimpse of her, but I was unsuccessful. Despite my efforts, I was unable to get close, even after running around to the back of the house multiple times.

The villagers shared stories of the deceased's kindness and generosity, but at that moment, such sentiments were distant to me. I longed to see Tulasi, but it seemed impossible. The police informed us that the body would be brought back in two days from the site of the incident. As evening fell, the crowd dispersed, leaving only close relatives by the house. Yet, I remained nearby, seated beneath the towering tree, consumed by sorrow and regret."

"It was midnight," Vishwa continues, "and I stood quietly in the backyard of Tulasi's house. I hadn't sent her any message to meet me, but an unknown confidence told me she would come to me again that night. The lights in the house were still on, indicating that people hadn't yet retired for the night. My mind was awash with countless thoughts, and I knew I couldn't calm them until I saw Tulasi. I hoped and prayed a thousand times that she would be alright and find the courage to overcome the tragedy.

As time passed, hour by hour, a multitude of thoughts swirled through my mind, each one adding to the uncertainty of whether Tulasi would come to me that night. My confidence in her arrival diminished with every passing hour, and I couldn't help but wonder how she was coping with the tragedy. Until then, I had only experienced physical relationships with young girls and married women, never taking the time to understand their inner selves or consider their feelings. I had never truly grasped what marriage meant to them or the complexities they faced. Doubts and questions filled my mind as dawn approached, and eventually, I lost hope in waiting any longer. Before my presence could become a sensation in the village, I quietly slipped away through the trees and returned home.

The next morning, I resumed my routine of waiting near Tulasi's house, hoping to catch a glimpse of her. As I scanned the front yard, I suddenly noticed a woman carrying out morning household tasks—it was Tulasi. However, she seemed preoccupied, focused on her chores. Despite my urge to call out to her, I remained silent, feeling powerless. In a moment of desperation, I picked up a stone and hurled it into the branches of the tree above me, startling the birds into flight. Tulasi turned towards the tree, her gaze meeting mine. The desolation in her eyes struck me deeply—it was a look I would never forget, even in my dreams. Her face was devoid of expression, and tears silently traced down her cheeks before she turned away and disappeared into the house. I continued to watch her, trying to understand the meaning behind her gaze, but I realised then that I could never truly comprehend the emotions of a married woman, no matter how much I loved her. I didn't act impulsively; instead, I observed her with empathy.

The next evening was the time set for the arrival of his deceased body. After witnessing Tulasi's desolate look, I refrained from approaching her again as I grappled with the meaning behind her expression. I decided not to be present when her husband's body arrived, as I didn't want to witness her emotions firsthand. However, nearly the entire village gathered outside Tulasi's house to await the arrival. I observed her grieving for her husband, and I realised she was not an emotionless stone. Honestly, my thoughts wandered to how long she would remain in mourning, as I believed that the only barrier between us had been divinely removed. I prayed fervently for her to find the strength to overcome her sorrow and move past this ordeal as swiftly as possible.

My mind wandered wildly, envisioning a future with Tulasi. I entertained the audacious idea of claiming her hand after her husband's passing, believing I could convince both families to accept our union. Yet, beneath my seemingly noble intentions lay a selfish desire, deriving a perverse pleasure from the misfortune that had befallen her. The truth of my character revealed itself in the face of adversity, exposing my innermost thoughts and motivations.

I ventured out that night and sought refuge in alcohol, hoping to quell the storm of emotions raging within me.

Later that night, upon returning home, I heard the horrifying news that shattered my world. My parents had just returned from Tulasi's house and recounted the tragic events. As Tulasi gazed upon her deceased husband's face, she collapsed and died upon his body. I couldn't comprehend what I was hearing. My mind refused to accept the news, rendering my body numb and unresponsive. After my father repeated the news three times, I bolted towards her house.

I ran blindly, recklessly, colliding with trees and obstacles along the way, consumed by a singular purpose: to reach Tulasi."

Vishwa continues his narrative, his voice heavy with the weight of sorrowful memories. "By the time I reached there, the front yard was crowded with villagers who seemed determined not to leave that night. Pushing through the throng, I made my way to where two coffins lay side by side. A profound emptiness gripped me, numbing my senses. Everything around me faded into insignificance. I wanted to kneel before her, to grasp her feet, but I was paralysed by the enormity of the moment.

When I saw Tulasi's face, the meaning of her desolate expression from the day before became clear to me—it was guilt. She was consumed by guilt, tormented by the weight of her actions. For the first time, I felt I could truly empathise with her plight. She must have felt overwhelming remorse for her infidelity while her husband selflessly served the nation. I imagine her guilt as a sword piercing her unfaithful heart.

I don't dare ask for her forgiveness. Instead, I pray fervently to God, begging for the harshest punishment for my grave transgressions and for granting her eternal peace in heaven."

As Vishwa finishes his story, the night envelops us in its darkness, filled with the symphony of jungle sounds and the rushing stream. My heart feels heavy, weighed down by the profound tragedy of his tale. Without a word, Vishwa abruptly begins running up the steps, with Kalyani following closely behind. I understand that this is how he coped—with relentless determination to overcome the deepest anguish of his life. It was a testament to his resilience.

Before we board the Beast, I approach Vishwa and embrace him tightly, patting his back affectionately. In this juncture, I feel a profound admiration for his strength and resilience in the face of overwhelming grief.

We embark on our journey through dark, heavily forested roads, with only the dim headlights illuminating a partial view of the path ahead. The silence inside the jeep is palpable, matching the grim mood of our surroundings. Kalyani eventually pulls over at a chai point slightly off the road, offering a momentary respite from the intense atmosphere. While sipping on the native tea, Kalyani begins recounting the concluding part of Vishwa's story.

"Knowing Vishwa's culpability in Tulasi's tragic death, his family decided to leave the village, burdened with the weight of guilt. Before departing, his father imposed a punishment on him—he was forbidden to leave the village until he received forgiveness from his family."

Now, we find ourselves at a secluded house surrounded by a two-acre agricultural plot. Warmly welcomed by elderly residents and a few children in the front yard, I am filled with a sense of delight. After a tour of the property, we are treated to a simple yet flavorful dinner prepared with vegetables grown organically on their farm.

"Vishwa was tormented in hell for a year," Kalyani narrates. "Later, his inherently strong character drove him to give back to society, a way of begging forgiveness. He transformed his house and farm into an orphanage for destitute young children and abandoned elderly in the region, naming it after Tulasi. He dedicated his life to this mission, living an ascetic existence to atone for his love for Tulasi's peacefulness. Vishwa had been a vagabond before she entered his life, but after her passing, he became responsible and committed to working on his farm alongside others. He began crafting various handicrafts that garnered demand in tourist destinations like Araku and even exported them to larger markets in the city. All the earnings were channelled into the well-being of everyone at Tulasi's home."

The joy radiating from the children here is striking, a happiness that seems elusive even among the affluent in the city. Instantly, I feel a strong urge to contribute something meaningful to their lives when I achieve success. Meanwhile, Kalyani engages in a serious conversation with Vishwa indoors, visible through a nearby window. Unsure of their discussion, I turn my attention to the people around me.

As I mingle with the cheerful residents on the veranda, a man emerges from the dark entrance, clearly inebriated. Despite the protests of two elderly women urging him to leave, he clumsily approaches the veranda, inadvertently causing a commotion by knocking over some vessels. The noise draws everyone's attention, prompting the inhabitants of the home to step outside, curious about the disturbance.

"Come out, you coward! I will not leave this place before I kill you tonight," the intoxicated man shouts with angry pauses, his voice echoing across the quiet surroundings. He repeatedly calls out for someone as the residents gather on the veranda to see what's happening.

Vishwa steps out to assess the situation, but an old woman stops him by grabbing his hand. He looks at her with determination and says, "The punishment I deserve awaits me there. Evading it doesn't diminish the sins I have committed. Please let me go, mother!" Reluctantly, the old lady releases him, and Vishwa walks out into the open.

The drunken man, fueled by rage, approaches Vishwa and begins to slap him forcefully across the face. I am shocked by the lack of intervention as the man continues to assault Vishwa, shouting, "Die, you bastard, for killing my sister! You are dying tonight in my hands." His words punctuate each blow, the violence escalating until the man collapses from exhaustion.

Quietly bearing the humiliation, Vishwa returns inside the home with his head bowed. Despite offers of help from a couple of elderly residents, he declines. Kalyani and I exchange looks of concern as she approaches me and explains that the man is Tulasi's elder brother, prone to violent outbursts when intoxicated. She adds, "Though there's no evidence of your crimes, everyone in this small village knows what must have happened."

As Vishwa sees us off on the road, I notice multiple bruises on his face, which he refuses to treat.

"Why?" Kalyani asks him once we're settled in the driver's seat, and I watch Vishwa closely for his response.

"It is this punishment that makes me feel justified for my sins, at least a little. An unpunished sin only increases your suffering," Vishwa replies solemnly, his words echoing in my mind as the Beast carries us onto the main road in search of accommodation for the night.

"Actually, this has been bothering me since I met him. How did you meet him, and how did you two become friends?" I ask Kalyani eagerly.

"Ha ha... that's a long story. I'll share it when the time is right. You've heard enough stories for today," Kalyani responds with a wide smile. She refocuses on driving as we continue toward Araku through the winding ghat road, enveloped in darkness without streetlights.

*****

We find ourselves in a spacious, double-sized room on the first floor of a newly constructed resort, a bit removed from the main road of Araku. Kalyani opted for this room due to her dissatisfaction with the cleanliness of standard accommodations, particularly the bathrooms. Upon arrival, her first action is to inspect the bathroom while I take care of opening the curtains to reveal a wide glass window beside the large bed. The room is tastefully furnished with an L-shaped sofa in one corner, a glass teapoy, and two additional chairs, much to our satisfaction.

After freshening up, I settle onto the sofa and watch as Kalyani emerges from the bathroom wearing a pale beige saree. Standing before the tall mirror near the door, she adjusts her attire with meticulous care. Her appearance is striking in this new ensemble, and I find myself stealing glances at her repeatedly. As she wipes her damp hair and lays a towel over a chair to dry, she wrestles with her unruly locks, attempting to tame them into a neat plait. My eyes wander to the golden triangle formed at her side waist between the maroon blouse and the saree—a detail that captivates me, considering my unfamiliarity with this traditional attire. Kalyani effortlessly introduces me to this new world of elegance, showcasing her own unique beauty.

Yet, my thoughts are continually interrupted by unwelcome flashes of her provocative expressions from the scandalous video. Despite her charm, I cannot shake the image of her involvement in such a calamitous act of adultery. I ponder what might have been—perhaps a dignified lady of a respected family— if not for her indiscretion with that man.

As I contemplate various thoughts, Kalyani slowly moves to the bed, steps onto it, and settles in the middle, cross-legged, facing the wide glass window that offers a captivating view of the village adorned with dazzling lights. Positioned behind her on the sofa, I lean to the left to get a better view. With her hands resting on her knees and her eyes closed in a serene posture, it appears she is meditating or perhaps engaged in some form of penance.

Fascinated by this sight, I approach the window, struck by the beauty of this lady in a saree, assuming such a peaceful stance. I recall how she referred to me as a saint when she witnessed me in a similar posture during our time at the police station. *"You cannot recognise another saint unless you are one yourself,"* I muse silently.

Returning to the sofa, I remain quiet, not wanting to disturb the tranquil aura she seems to be cultivating through her meditation. I've heard that positive waves generated during meditation can be beneficial if one remains still in proximity. As I observe her in this graceful pose, her physical beauty fades into the background, replaced by a profound impact on my perception of her.

Despite the serene scene, questions begin to surface in my mind. *"Why has Kalyani never shared anything about her past with me? I'm tempted to confront her about the scandalous video I stumbled upon, desperate for clarity and closure regarding her history. Confronting her about this could be the key to moving past the persisting shadow of Saira that hangs over me. I wonder if seeking companionship with another*

She opens her eyes and relaxes her body from the stiff, erect position. Getting off the bed, she takes her phone to check for any messages and then announces, "Hey, we have got the network here. You've been waiting for it, haven't you?"

"Yes, I have. But I no longer need it now," I respond calmly.

"What? Why do you think that?" Kalyani looks surprised as we sit on adjacent sides of the L-shaped sofa, unpacking the food brought by the attendant. As I arrange chapati and curry on our plates, I prepare my response.

"Well, I've come to realise something. I've seen various websites and YouTube channels talking about conspiring with the universe, proposing techniques to make things happen by harnessing the power of your wishes. Some even claim you can 'attract the person you love' using these methods. But I find it all quite selfish, because if you're forcing someone to love you, how can it be called love?"

"I don't quite follow," Kalyani responds.

"Imagine if I tried to persuade Saira to come back to me using these techniques. It's like pulling her towards me against her will," I explain.

Kalyani's left eyebrow raises, indicating her growing understanding.

"True love should be freely chosen by both parties. If someone truly wants to be with you, they'll choose to do so of their own accord, not because of some cosmic manipulation or convincing tactics. Otherwise, it's not love; it's just manipulation. Do you know what I admire most about my relationship with Saira?"

"I'm listening," Kalyani prompts.

"Neither of us had ever tried to impress each other, nor had we proposed for a hand. It was from two free-willed hearts that we started sharing life. The way we looked at each other whenever we met initially, those looks were clear in conveying the message to our souls, craving a bond that would never cease. And..."

"But can't you see it as a way to reconcile with her after a tussle or a serious fight? Isn't it your responsibility to communicate with her about how much you love her?" Kalyani interjects.

"Indeed, my attempts to reach out to her ended shortly after our separation began. I reached a point where I had expressed everything I needed to say, and I'm certain she understood the depth of my feelings for her. Despite this, she decided to stay away from my life and does not want to communicate with me anymore. Why then did I try so hard to persuade her? There's no use in convincing someone who fully comprehends the extent of your emotions toward them. She knew she was central to my life—though I hesitate to call it 'my' life. Still, she chose to depart. I must allow her to lead her own life without my influence. I do not wish to push her back into my world through the power of my words. Let her be the master of her own thoughts and destiny."

"I understand," Kalyani responds.

"All I am struggling with is to find a way to love her without reaching her because I cannot hate her by any means. Despite everything, I can only love her. My life is merely what happened during those six years. I think that's the end of any significant time of mine. I pray to the universe with all my senses to not disturb her free will and her whole-hearted wishes."

"You will not disappoint me in being called a saint. Truly, you are one," Kalyani remarks.

"Come on! I am struggling hard to survive being an ordinary human. I don't know about being a saint."

As we are immersed in our conversation, I hear the pleading cry of a girl from somewhere nearby. Kalyani also hears the sound and suddenly becomes alert. It must be the voice of a young girl coming from a room across the corridor. We tend to ignore it initially, assuming it's common to have guests in the hotel. However, the shrill cry continues, growing more emotional and desperate. Suddenly, we hear the sound of two heavy slaps, and the girl's cry becomes louder.

Kalyani's expression turns to anger, and she rises from the sofa, moving towards the door to listen more closely. I follow her quietly as we stand behind the door, waiting to understand the situation. Laughter from men echoes down the corridor, contrasting sharply with the girl's cries.

We exchange a determined glance with each other, both aware that some serious action may be necessary.

Chapter 7: Sins of the Past

"How dare you deny me, you filthy bitch? You should have known what this work entails before coming here. Come on, come forward and do it!" growls a menacing male voice, followed by a thud and the trembling cries of the girl, indicating that she is being severely beaten. The desperation in her voice is palpable as she pleads to be left alone.

Kalyani and I lurk behind the door, strategising how to confront the situation. Kalyani silently counts the number of men, preparing for a potential physical confrontation. I am amazed by her courage and determination to face them head-on. Though unsure of what to do, I intend to stand by her side no matter the outcome. I am deeply impressed by her bravery in risking herself to save the girl. She must know the risks if we are outnumbered, yet she is determined to intervene.

Suddenly, a knock on the door interrupts our thoughts. It's the reception boy delivering alcohol and cigarettes. Kalyani opens the door to receive the items, seizing the opportunity to engage him in conversation, hoping to glean more information about the commotion down the corridor. Peering through the partially open door, I can see the corridor and the rooms opposite. To our surprise, all those rooms are locked, confirming that the girl's voice is indeed coming from a room around the left corner.

The girl's pleas grow clearer, echoing down the corridor as she continues to beg for release. The attendant appears indifferent to the situation, merely apologising for the delay before leaving. Kalyani closes the door decisively and declares, "We must stop them from assaulting her." Her unwavering gaze locks with mine, conveying her determination. "I'm not certain how many men there are, but we have to act."

As we prepare to intervene, the gravity of the situation weighs heavily on us. Kalyani's resolve and determination inspire a sense of purpose within me, igniting a shared determination to protect the vulnerable girl from harm.

She goes to the end of the corridor and lurks at the turn to observe the men. I follow her and stand behind her.

"There's a party of four men sitting around a girl in front of a room. It's outside in the corridor, so it is not impossible." She asserts. I ask her to move aside so that I can also have a glimpse of the scene. As I sneak from behind the wall, I see that only one room is brightly lit in the corridor, and it is the second room after the turn. The scene looks barbaric in the way the girl is lying on a man's lap with her hands tightly held by him. The four men are young and in their early twenties. One of the two sitting at her legs is holding a mobile phone in his hands to shoot her assault. He announces them to "start".

We rush to them from the corner as each one of them looks startled. The sudden interference of others has literally shocked them. The teenage girl has stopped crying and is giving us an imploring look to save her. But the man holding her is fastening his grip on her hands. Some are without shirts, and the man dealing with her is only wearing shorts. Kalyani shouts at them straight away and demands them in an authoritative tone to leave the girl. They all burst out in sarcastic laughter instantly. Two of them whoop in joy, and a man yells, "A lady in a beautiful sari at this time in the hotel. I know who you are, *randi*. Why don't you join us for the night? Your succulent fruits will be far more delicious than that of this little bitch lying down here. Don't worry! We will pay you double the amount he's got you for."

"Leave her at once!" She demands.

"She'll be there as a side dish, don't worry, dear. Come on in, you slut!" the young one gets up to hold Kalyani's hand.

A man on the right attempts to snatch Kalyani's hand forcefully. She instinctively raises her arm to defend herself, driving her elbow into his chest with a powerful blow that brings him to his knees. This sudden action startles the other three men, their collective anger uniting them to seize hold of Kalyani, leaving the young girl on the floor.

Despite my efforts, I struggle to free Kalyani from their grasp. They restrain her tightly, each man gripping one of her hands and another around her waist, pulling her towards the room despite her resistance. Their anger is evident in their abusive words towards her.

I desperately attempt to intervene, but I am outnumbered and overpowered. Two of them possess substantial strength with muscular builds, while the other two are lean yet towering. Fear grips me as I realise the daunting challenge of confronting them in this dire situation.

As I contemplate our predicament, Kalyani is already being dragged into the room. She fights relentlessly, striking out with whatever part of her body she can free. However, she is soon subdued by the two burly men—one pinning her arms tightly against the wall, while the other restricts her legs.

Meanwhile, I am held firmly by two men, my arms twisted behind my back and an arm around my neck, making it difficult to move or resist. Behind me, the young girl cautiously lurks at the room's entrance, retrieving her dupatta from the floor to cover herself. The tension in the air is palpable as we face the grim reality of our captivity.

"This is what I always wanted to have…" The fifth man sitting in the corner of the room extols Kalyani's body by passing lustrous glances at her various parts.

"Who would miss an opportunity to enjoy a voluptuous beauty like this? And you brought that little bitch who is still to display her assets. Now I'm ready with this one." The fifth man, who appears to be a middle-aged and more experienced one in the group, comes close to her.

"It's been a long time, dear! How the hell could you come here? By any chance, are you still in search of me? Wow! This is a really big night for all of us to relish you. You will not close your eyes till the first light in the morning." The middle-aged man grins widely and is followed by all the other men. He reaches her body in the closest proximity and feels her chest from an inch distance. "Let me take the cover off the most beautiful pair of things that you might see in your life." He announces by placing his hand on the upper part of her *pallu.* Kalyani looks at him, whom she identifies from her past. I don't know what sort of history they share, but I see them having a strong connection. With a sudden jolt, he pulls it off by cutting its pin link from her blouse. The pull is so powerful that even the edge of the blouse on her shoulder is torn over an inch. It makes visible the cleavage of her bosoms. Below her blouse, the golden part of her hip and her navel at its centre are uncovered.

I am filled with a sense of helplessness as I witness the horrifying ordeal unfolding before me. My anger boils over, and I yell at the attackers with all the fury I can muster. Kalyani, fueled by rage, unleashes her power, struggling against the men who have seized her. Despite their hold, she manages to raise her legs, striking out forcefully in defence.

I am awestruck by Kalyani's courageous resistance against the assailants. They press her tightly against the wall, their touch filled with malicious intent, while the fifth man callously pulls her blouse, exposing her pink bra and half of her breasts. The other men revel in this disgraceful display, laughing cruelly and eagerly anticipating more.

Desperate to break free, I exert all my strength against the grip of the young man restraining me. Meanwhile, the middle-aged man crosses another boundary, cupping Kalyani's breast and nearly touching it through her blouse. This unbearable violation triggers a surge of determination within Kalyani.

In a moment of sheer defiance, Kalyani delivers a devastating blow to the man's groin with her raised leg, causing him to collapse in pain. Seizing the opportunity, I wrench myself free from the young man's grip and swiftly strike back, targeting the other assailants with all my might.

I deliver a powerful blow to one of the young man's groins, leaving him incapacitated on the floor, followed by another impactful strike to the other man, rendering them both helpless. Kneeling and clutching their lower parts in agony, they are unable to stand.

Meanwhile, Kalyani grabs a steel pipe from the window curtain, wielding it like a weapon, striking the attackers relentlessly. I seize a wine bottle from the nearby table, smashing it against their heads one by one. The impact shatters the glass, causing two of them to bleed profusely from their wounds.

The chaos and violence escalate as we fight back ferociously, driven by sheer determination to defend ourselves against these despicable attackers.

Emerging from the room in a rush, I quickly bolt the door from the outside, trapping all the men inside. Together with the young girl, we hastily retreat to our room, frantically packing our belongings. Kalyani adjusts her pallu to cover her half-exposed breasts and joins me in gathering our clothes and any open refreshments left on the table.

Filled with adrenaline and fear, I stuff our belongings into my backpack, experiencing an overwhelming sense of urgency to escape before the men emerge from their room in pursuit. There's no time for thorough packing; we grab whatever we can see without hesitation.

The young girl positions herself at the corner of the corridor, keeping watch for any sign of the men leaving their room, ready to warn us if necessary. With a sense of urgency, we finish gathering our things and rush out into the corridor, locking our room behind us.

I call the young girl to follow us as we race down the staircase and out of the resort. At the reception desk, I hastily drop off my key before joining Kalyani and the girl outside. Without waiting for any acknowledgement from the receptionist, I make my way to the main entrance.

Within moments, the three of us are speeding away in our vehicle, aptly named "the Beast," racing down the road away from the resort. As we leave the confines of the resort behind, I catch sight of my underwear left hanging in the window to dry.

As our vehicle raccs away from the town centre, each passing kilometre carries us further from the chaos left behind. The landscape transforms around us, the familiar town giving way to quiet hamlets and the winding path promising concealment. Kalyani manoeuvres into a narrow, dark path on the right, her quick thinking under pressure evident in the calculated move to throw off any pursuers.

Inside the vehicle, the atmosphere is heavy with unspoken tension. Kalyani, usually vibrant and expressive, falls uncharacteristically silent, her eyes fixed ahead as if processing the recent events. I, too, sit in contemplative silence, grappling with the adrenaline-fueled aftermath of the encounter.

As we come to a stop near the hillside houses, a sense of stillness settles around us. The moonlight bathes the landscape in a surreal glow, casting shadows that dance across the terrain. Amid this tranquil scene, the young girl sits beside us, visibly shaken and exhausted from the ordeal.

In this moment of respite, the air is charged with a mix of relief and lingering apprehension. We are safe for now, but the events of the night have left an indelible mark, a testament to the unpredictable nature of the world we navigate together.

"You two stay here for a while. I've forgotten something in town. I'll go and collect it," Kalyani says with a troubled expression on her face. It's clear that her mission is somehow connected to the man from the room, someone she knew from her past.

"But it's too dangerous to go back to them now. Please listen to me. Whatever history you have with him, we won't stand a chance if we face them again," I plead with Kalyani, noticing her constant backwards glances filled with anger. I can sense her overwhelming desire for revenge. "Was he someone from your past?" I ask cautiously.

"He *was* my past," Kalyani responds, her rage evident as she grips the steering wheel tightly, her hands trembling with fury. There's a sudden thump as she curses both him and herself for leaving him unpunished.

"I, too, want to see him suffer, but the two of us alone won't be enough for this task. Besides, they're probably on alert by now. It's too risky to go back," I reason with her.

"Let's not talk about that now. Look, there's a tea stall nearby if we need something," Kalyani suggests, stepping out of the Beast. She turns to the back seat, focusing on our responsibility to the young girl.

"What's your name?" Kalyani's voice softens as she addresses the fragile girl sitting in the back seat.

"M... M... Mallika," comes the trembling reply.

"Don't worry, Mallika. We'll take you to your parents. Where do you live?" Kalyani asks gently.

Mallika blinks her innocent eyes a few times before responding in a soft voice, "My parents are no more."

"Alas! Then who do you stay with?" Kalyani inquires further.

"With my uncle and aunt in a village on the other side of Araku. They sent me for this work, promising to send me to school if I earn money at night," Mallika explains, her voice tinged with sadness.

"Do you want to go back to them?" Kalyani asks, her tone filled with empathy.

"No, please take me somewhere else. I can do all kinds of household work. Please help me," Mallika sobs, hiding her face between her knees.

Moved by Mallika's plight, Kalyani and I exchange a solemn glance, silently determined to protect and guide her to safety.

Kalyani and I share a compassionate glance, and then Kalyani assures Mallika, "Don't worry. We'll take you to a place where you can work and continue your studies."

I understand that Kalyani has decided to take Mallika to Tulasi's home, a haven for young girls like her.

"We'll sort everything out first thing in the morning. For now, rest and relax. Have you eaten anything, dear?" Kalyani asks Mallika, noticing tears streaming down her cheeks.

"No…" Mallika responds softly, her hunger evident.

Kalyani takes out a wrapped pack of khichdi from her bag and offers it to Mallika. "Come on, eat, sweetheart! You have a long journey ahead in life. Don't exhaust yourself here."

Mallika eagerly opens the pack and starts devouring each morsel, while Kalyani and I exchange glances, struck by the extent of her hunger. Kalyani passes a water bottle to Mallika in the back seat, ensuring she has something to drink along with her meal.

As Mallika eats, I find myself gazing out through the windshield into the wilderness. The near-full moon on this foggy night fails to conceal the captivating beauty of nature. The valley unfolds before me, its landscape enchanting and serene. I'm drawn to the scintillating sight of the hillside leading down into a ravine. In the distance, a small hamlet near the ravine twinkles with lights, casting a warm glow on both sides of the stream.

Amidst the challenges and uncertainties of the night, the beauty of the landscape offers a moment of solace and wonder, a reminder of the stability and quiet strength that nature embodies.

*****

I find myself immersed in a journey I never anticipated, each moment feeling like a dream that might fade at any instant. Here we are, gathered around a small fire beside the road, an unlikely group brought together by circumstance. Kalyani, ever resourceful, has struck up a quick friendship with an elderly man at a modest tea stall, which is also stuffed with essential items for the villagers. Now he's graciously shared his tea with us.

In her characteristic generosity, Kalyani has reciprocated by offering our refreshments and alcohol to our newfound companion. Now, under the glow of the firelight, we sit together, sipping our drinks and exchanging stories around the crackling of the flames.

As I glance around at our eclectic assembly, I'm struck by the fascinating mix of personalities fate has assembled here. There's the elderly man, his weathered face telling stories of a lifetime spent in this quiet corner of the world. Beside him sits Mallika, a young girl thrust into uncertainty, her tear-stained face a testament to the challenges she faces. Then there's Kalyani, a pillar of strength and resilience, exuding a sense of calm authority even in adversity.

And then there's me, navigating through my own personal struggles and recently rescued from the depths of guilt by these unexpected allies. It's a scene that feels straight out of a novel, a tapestry of human experiences woven together under the canvas of the night sky.

Kalyani's question breaks the reverie, her mischievous grin inviting a playful response. "Do you know how to fight?" she asks, her eyes twinkling with amusement. I sense her teasing tone, an acknowledgement of the events that brought us together.

At that moment, I'm struck by Kalyani's presence. Despite the recent ordeal, she exudes a captivating sense of grace and authenticity. Her demeanour, from the way she wears her saree with dignity to her genuine concern for others, sets her apart from anyone I've known.

As the fire crackles and the night unfolds around us, I can't help but marvel at the unexpected beauty of this shared moment. It's a reminder of the unpredictable nature of life and the profound connections that can arise when least expected.

Two hours pass by in a blur of conversation and companionship, each moment becoming more cherished as time slips away unnoticed. Mallika, overcome with weariness, retreats to the Beast and curls up on the back seat. Kalyani, ever attentive, covers her with the sole blanket available, her generosity touching me deeply.

Watching Mallika drift into sleep, Kalyani and I return to the dying embers of the campfire, our glasses still in hand. Kalyani shares another round of drinks with the man, savouring the warmth of the fire against the cool night air. Kalyani didn't force me after I had shaken my head when offered the first peg earlier. Soon, the elderly man, sensing the late hour, bids us goodnight and makes his way to his humble hut, where he must rise early to prepare tea for his regular customers.

Left alone by the dwindling firelight, Kalyani lights a cigarette and passes it to me. The first puff of smoke escapes her lips like a wisp of ethereal energy, captivating me with its allure. I find myself entranced by the sight of her, the cigarette in her hand adding to her mystique.

Taking a drag from the cigarette she offers, I marvel at the complexities of human nature and the mysteries of attraction. There's an inexplicable fascination I feel towards women who smoke, a mixture of rebellion and allure that defies explanation.

As Kalyani indulges in her cigarette, her gaze drifts towards the distant village twinkling on the hillside like a constellation of white dots.

"What's so special about that village?" I inquire, intrigued by her sudden contemplation.

With a deep sigh, Kalyani opens up, revealing a glimpse of her past. "It's my village, the place where I was born and brought up," she begins, her voice carrying a hint of nostalgia and regret. "I lived there until I disgraced my family. I had to leave because of choices I made in my teenage years, choices that I deeply regret."

I listen intently as Kalyani begins to unravel her past, her voice carrying a mix of nostalgia and remorse. The moonlight casts a serene glow over the surroundings, enhancing the solemnity of her revelations.

"I have wonderful parents," she begins, her tone wistful. "I am their first child, and they gave me everything I asked for. They agreed to my education in a junior college in Araku town, and we used to walk up the hill before catching an auto to the college. That road was just a walking path back then. It was during this time that a young man in his mid-twenties entered my life as a responsible auto driver."

"Was that man the same middle-aged person we encountered at the resort tonight?" I inquire, trying to piece together the puzzle.

"Yes, he's the one who destroyed everything and led my life to ruin," Kalyani responds with a heavy sigh. "You must have noticed the way I looked at him in that room."

"Indeed, I sensed the tension between you," I acknowledge.

"No, I misspoke earlier. He didn't destroy everything outright; he lured me towards a path of calamity," Kalyani clarifies. "His name is Vinod. I fell deeply in love with him before I even turned eighteen. As a diligent student in my first year of Junior college, I transformed into a reckless young girl who preferred wandering in the woods with him over attending classes. I was consumed by thoughts of him, neglecting my family and my younger sister."

I study Kalyani's expression closely, searching for traces of tears, but her eyes reflect a deep sense of resignation. Her desolate gaze suggests that her tears dried up long ago, leaving behind scars that have since hardened.

"I was a rebel at heart," Kalyani admits with a rueful smile. "My parents wanted me to settle down with someone else, but Vinod stood by me and encouraged me to break free. We envisioned a blissful life together outside my family home. I refused to leave without getting married, so we wedded hastily in a temple on the hill."

"You got married and lived together?" I ask, surprised by the spontaneity of their union.

"I insisted on it. I trusted him completely. I managed to secure admission to an engineering college near the city," she continues, her voice tinged with regret. "Vinod started working as an auto driver there. I was determined to prove myself and achieve success. I envisioned a future where I could proudly introduce him to my family, perhaps with a child by my side."

Kalyani explains further, "But our newfound freedom led us down the path of sensuality. We indulged in our desires day and night, neglecting my original ambitions of studying further with his support."

As Kalyani recounts her tumultuous past, I listen intently, my mind flooded with fleeting glimpses of my romantic history, each detail resonating with familiar echoes.

"My interest in education gradually receded, replaced by an overwhelming craving for his touch and the surge of our shared sexual fantasies," Kalyani confesses. "During that time, nothing else seemed to matter as much to me. Being with him felt like heaven, and I was deeply under his influence, unable to recognise his flaws. What might have seemed eccentric or unusual became normal to me within the context of our relationship. This trance-like state persisted for almost a year.

Gradually, Vinod began revealing his true colours through his habits and the company he kept, especially his friends who showed inappropriate interest in me, which he seemed unconcerned about. He started engaging in cricket betting and eventually abandoned his auto-rickshaw work. Vinod tried to convince me to drop out of college, insisting that his newfound earnings were sufficient. Fed up with his lifestyle, I finally left our home one day and decided to return to my parents, willing to face whatever punishment awaited me.

As I waited at the railway station for my train back to Araku, Vinod bombarded my phone with multiple calls that I intentionally ignored. Finally, when my train arrived, and I settled into a seat by the window, I received a shocking video message on WhatsApp. Opening it, I was confronted with a self-shot video clip of our intimate moments from the early days of our marriage. It was a devastating realisation of how deeply entangled I had become in my self-created troubles."

Her story unfolds like a cautionary tale, a testament to the allure and dangers of youthful passion. As I listen, I can't help but reflect on my romantic escapades, mindful of the shadows that lurk beneath the surface of love's intoxicating facade.

Kalyani's expression turns solemn as she reminisces about her descent into a life she never imagined for herself. "With a blank and pale look, I moved to the doorway to get down," she continues, her voice tinged with regret. "That decision led me to rock bottom. I abandoned the idea of returning to my parents permanently. The shame of those videos circulating online stripped me of any sense of morality. Eventually, I became a pawn in Vinod's schemes, stooped to sleeping with his friends and strangers to settle his debts."

Her words weigh heavily on me as she reveals the dark reality of her existence. "I lost myself completely," she admits, her voice faltering. "I embraced a life of prostitution out of sheer survival, numbing myself to the pain and degradation. I disconnected from my roots, embracing the city as my new home and relishing the temporary comforts it offered."

As Kalyani's story unfolds, I'm struck by her resilience in adversity. "Much later, I met Bhasker sir, a CI in Bengaluru," she continues, a glimmer of hope in her eyes. "He saw me not as a fallen woman but as someone with potential. Under his guidance, I began to reclaim my self-respect, assisting him in gathering information on drug peddlers."

Kalyani's quest for redemption takes on a new urgency as she confides her desire for revenge against Vinod. "I've searched everywhere for him, but tonight is the first time I've come close," she explains, her gaze scanning the surroundings.

"What happened?" I inquire gently, seeking to understand her emotions.

Kalyani's voice carries a heavy weight of regret and longing as she reveals her internal struggle. "This road, which I take time to identify, indeed stands as a testimony to many of our casual encounters during the initial days of our romance," she explains, her tone tinged with bitterness. "I hate how much I craved his company back then. Returning here feels like completing a full circle, and I hope I never have to come back."

Her desire to shield her parents from the harsh truth of her current state adds another layer of complexity to her story. "Every nerve in me crushes with the urge to visit my parents in the village," she confesses, a tear glistening on her cheek in the faint light from the nearby tea shop. "But I dare not. They must still believe their daughter is happily married somewhere. I cannot shatter their dreams by revealing my brokenness."

A profound silence envelops us as we sit together in the Beast, contemplating the weight of Kalyani's words and the gravity of her unspoken pain.

Later, as exhaustion catches up with us, I find myself slipping into sleep in the front seats of the vehicle. Now, reflecting on my thoughts, I ponder silently. *"Can Kalyani never experience companionship with another man in the way normal women do?"* The question weighs heavily on my mind as I drift into a restless slumber, haunted by the enigmatic complexities of Kalyani's life and my own uncertainties about the future.

As I drift in my thoughts, two fireflies gracefully approach us inside the Jeep. Their sparkling lights dance around us like skiers on ice, drawing our attention. The fireflies land delicately on Kalyani, one perching on her head and the other just above the middle line of her breasts. They add a charming glow to Kalyani's already radiant beauty. Sensing the movement on her breasts, Kalyani adjusts her pallu slightly, inadvertently revealing the upper part of her bouncing breasts. The disturbance causes the two fireflies to flutter away, ending their brief visit.

As I reflect on the encounter, my mind wanders into deeper contemplation. *"I find myself questioning the influence of my upbringing on how I perceive a girl's sexuality. Did my exposure to Saira's uncovered beauty leave a lasting imprint on my mind and soul, making me morally conflicted? And now, after having glimpses of Kalyani during the hotel attack, am I feeling a similar sense of moral obligation towards her? I wonder if there's a direct correlation between seeing a girl naked and developing a desire to be with her. Does physical exposure truly matter in shaping our desires and connections? Whatever the reasons may be, I see this as a way to redeem myself from trying to pull Saira towards me. Perhaps Kalyani can provide the genuine diversion and connection I've been longing for."*

*****

I wake up to find the seat next to me empty, a slight concern nudging at my mind. *"Where is Kalyani"?* Stepping down from the Beast, I glance around, my eyes scanning the vicinity. Mallika is still nestled in the back seat, undisturbed in her sleep. Pacing a bit further, my gaze sweeps across the landscape until I spot

Kalyani emerging from a lower path. She's changed her attire, a brightness emanating from her countenance.

"Where have you been? I was worried," I express, my steps drawing closer to her.

"I know of a beautiful waterfall nearby. I wanted to cleanse myself one last time before we leave," she responds, her demeanour relaxed yet intriguing.

Her sudden declaration piques my curiosity further, her evident tranquillity unnerving me in a way.

"It's time for me to leave this place," she declares, her expression nuanced with subtle resolution.

Noticing the nuances on her face and her newfound serenity, I move to the opposite side of the road, ready to head to the fall.

"No, that one has very little water. I'll show you another spot, not far from here. Come along," she prompts, swiftly retreating into the Beast. Without a word, I follow suit, the engine rumbling to life.

Within minutes after dropping Mallika at Tulasi's Home, we arrive at another breathtaking waterfall. I marvel at the sheer exhilaration of drenching in the cascading stream, the morning sun shyly peeking through the clouds. The timing seems to have kept others at bay, granting us this serene playground of nature.

For an hour, we revel in the playful dance of water, hopping from one boulder to the next across the glistening stream. As fatigue gradually seeps into my limbs, I sense a profound rejuvenation coursing through my spirit. Reluctantly, we bid farewell to the waterfall, resuming our journey aboard the vehicle.

This moment encapsulates the captivating atmosphere crafted by the chilly drizzles enveloping the picturesque region of Araku. As we wind along the twisting roads, the sky remains shrouded in a veil of mist, concealing the majestic mountain summits that would ordinarily dominate the landscape. Instead, we are treated to a stunning sight of pale-hued mountains draped in ethereal fog, their contours softened and obscured by the dancing wisps of mist among the trees.

Kalyani, visibly captivated by the ambience, guides the Jeep along the road at a leisurely pace, almost as if she is relishing the profound essence of her surroundings. Despite our extended journey through this enchanting wilderness, neither of us feels the immediate urge to halt for food or tea. The rain continues unabated, its persistent rhythm adding to the dreamlike quality of our journey. The windshield wipers struggle against the deluge, their rhythmic swipes unable to keep pace with the downpour. Consequently, Kalyani manoeuvres the vehicle cautiously, navigating the slick road with a steady hand and a keen eye.

It's the afternoon, and we're still inside the Beast, surrounded by the relentless downpour. The front glass is obscured by water droplets, making it difficult to see the road clearly. Kalyani is driving cautiously, unable to rely on the wipers to keep up with the heavy rain. Throughout the day, we've been mesmerised by the captivating beauty of nature, forgetting to eat. Now, hunger gnaws at us.

We've been on the lookout for a decent restaurant, but the weather isn't cooperating. Every curve in the road brings the surprise of another vehicle heading in the opposite direction. Despite the challenging conditions, Kalyani is handling the driving admirably.

The nurturing motherly aspect of nature has transformed into a formidable force. The possibility of a heavy downpour increasing to the point of triggering landslides on the ghat road looms over us like a threat. We dare not stop anywhere, surrounded by hillsides that pose dangers. With great caution, we keep our eyes fixed on the road ahead, navigating through this challenging journey.

As the Jeep navigates a hairpin curve, a man suddenly comes into view standing beneath an umbrella on the hedge. Kalyani's keen eyes must have spotted him amidst the confusion of the heavy rain. She pulls over, and the man approaches the jeep, opening the back door and stepping inside with a leather bag in hand. He's dressed formally, with his shirt neatly tucked into his trousers.

At first glance, he exudes a professional demeanour, but his presence in this weather raises doubts in my mind. *"What is he doing here in this kind of weather? I* *thought we were the only ones from Bengaluru around here, "*I ponder silently, noting his attire, which appears similar to ours. Interestingly, he's wearing ordinary sandals, a contrast to what one might expect from a professional.

We respond with polite greetings in return for his thankful gesture.

"What brings you out in this odd weather?" Kalyani asks, taking the lead in our inquiries.

"I work in a private bank a few kilometres from here. I'm headed there now," he replies.

"You're going to work at this hour, in the afternoon?" I chime in, curious about his schedule.

"Newly married or what?" Kalyani adds with a touch of wit.

"I'm not married yet, but that's beside the point," he answers, unfazed. "I've already called workers to come early this morning. This is the best time for sowing. We are farmers."

His revelation prompts both of us to turn and regard him with a new respect.

"You work in agriculture, even with a job in hand?" I ask, intrigued.

"Nothing compares to farming. It's our true culture, not just a means of survival or earning money," he asserts firmly.

His conviction leaves us spellbound. *"For the first time, I've heard someone say that working is their culture. Have I ever felt this way while pursuing a job*

in the IT industry? Can I ever do something like that?"
My inner voice raises a series of questions.

"Don't you have a two-wheeler for your daily commute?" Kalyani asks further.

"I do, but I can't afford to risk any part of my body on these slippery roads during the rainy season. We fear it could make us unsuitable for agriculture permanently. We can't risk anything that hinders us from farming. If I have no other option but to use my vehicle, I'm ready to quit this job, but not farming," he explains earnestly.

As I listen to him, I reflect on his words. *"There's nothing else to know. It's a clear point about liberating our lives from the slavery of earning for a livelihood,"* I think to myself, exchanging looks with Kalyani, who seems to share my inner sentiment. She quietly shifts her attention back to the road, lost in her own thoughts.

"Please stop here. I'll get down," the man directs, pointing to a crossroad on the left. Kalyani pulls over, offering to drop him at his bank.

"Thank you, but there's no need. My bank is just a few yards off the road. Plus, your Jeep won't be able to make it down the muddy path," he declines politely.

With another round of thanks, the man exits the vehicle and closes the door behind him. Kalyani and I watch him with admiration until he disappears into the wilderness.

Chapter 8: Destiny

"*Life had never seemed so beautiful; every moment spent here felt truly blissful. Perhaps it was the divine ambience of the region, or maybe it was my lovely companion who showed me a completely new way of living. Our intimate conversations in the spots where we stayed, and the pure joy we experienced at every place we visited, will certainly be cherished forever in my heart. Yet, the one thing that weighs on my mind is that I have kept my diary, which I've been writing for days, hidden from Kalyani.*" These feelings stir within me.

My thoughts continue, *"Initially, my diary was a mere chronicle of my life shared with Saira. However, with the arrival of Kalyani's radiant soul into my desolate existence, my writing took on a new tone, and my perspective shifted. I no longer address anything to Saira, realising I will never see her again. I see myself as a complete zero compared to Saira's successful and happy life. I've always believed I don't deserve her. Our association was a blessing, and I dare not hope for more. I am prepared to remain below zero to keep my distance from her. When my mother suggested I travel around Vizag, I had no hesitation, knowing I would not encounter Saira in this region. Kalyani disrupts my train of thought when she returns with tea from a small café beside the restrooms she visited."*

"Where are you, saint?" Kalyani's assertive tone jolts me from my daydream.

"Not so far away that you can't bring me back," I respond.

She silently slides into the driver's seat, and within moments, we're cruising down the main road toward the town center. It's a late sunny afternoon, just past four o'clock—a perfect time for nature enthusiasts to emerge from their cozy beds and explore the region. The rain had cleared up about half an hour ago, and we're cruising down the main road after a short tea break.

As the car speeds along, I steal glances at Kalyani. She's unusually quiet. I try to engage her in conversation, but her true self seems absent. It's clear she's lost in thought, the vehicle's speed reflecting her inner turmoil. She rarely drives so fast, let alone in silence. I've never seen her ponder deeply about anything.

Unable to bear her unusual behaviour, I gently place my right hand on her left one. The touch seems to rouse her from profound contemplation, her eyelids fluttering as she attempts to suppress something stirring within.

"You know, in a relationship, it's often the one who invests more—the one who truly puts their heart and soul into it—that ends up suffering," Kalyani shares her perspective on love, her voice carrying a hint of cynicism.

"It's not simply about loving deeply and having expectations; it's about the other person deserving the love you give," she continues, her words resonating deeply within me.

Her statement stirs a wave of self-reflection. *"I believe Saira left because I never truly deserved her,"* I admit softly. *"I cherished every moment we shared, but now, looking back, I struggle to recall any significant gestures or acts of kindness that I bestowed upon her. There's no point in dwelling on her departure from the desolate landscape of my existence."*

As I dwell on these thoughts, memories of our time together flood my mind, each one a poignant reminder of a story that had once felt whole and complete.

"Take my own story, for instance," Kalyani begins, noticing my downcast expression filled with guilt.

"Yes, I was too submissive to his manipulations to hold him accountable for anything," she continues. "The first time Vinod showed me an adult website with four of our video clips available to download or play, my heart shattered into uncontrollable tears. The devastation was unimaginable. I saw him suffering too, which only deepened my misplaced trust in him."

As our conversation deepens, she pulls the car over beneath a sprawling tree that bends over, casting a canopy across the road. A small rivulet trickles nearby, its gentle sound greeting us instantly. Silence settles around us, allowing my senses to absorb the intricate details of our surroundings.

Beyond what I see, I feel a poignant sense of longing for my happier self, a stark contrast to the journey to Araku. Surrounded by strangers, I find myself missing Saira at every stop. *"Oh no! Her absence has engulfed me so deeply that I've begun missing the person I used to be, who also misses her deeply."*

"It was my first love," she continues, her voice heavy with emotion. "I gave myself every chance to believe he could change for the better. Instead, he took advantage of me in every possible way. Gradually, I lost my true self, realising too late that I had become his slave. He left me in a state of desolation and disappeared."

I listen intently to Kalyani, trying to grasp the harrowing reality behind her cryptic and abstract explanations.

"As you know, he filmed us making love, with my consent, not with a hidden camera. I loved him so deeply and completely that nothing seemed suspicious. Then he claimed that his friends had uploaded the video to the adult website, but assured me they could have it removed since they were supposedly experts," she reveals, lighting a cigarette as if needing the comfort to reveal more painful truths.

"After a few puffs, she continues, "He manipulated me into going to their room with him under the guise of seeking their help. They offered us drinks, and I became completely intoxicated. He then left on an urgent call, leaving me vulnerable. That's when three of his friends sexually assaulted me, and I was powerless to stop them. They recorded the assault and began blackmailing me. He continued to feign innocence throughout. They used him as a tool to exploit me further, sending me to satisfy the needs of high-profile individuals. At that point, I was seduced by the allure of money and luxury. I was numbed by comfort and trapped."

Tears glisten on her cheeks, a stark contrast to the image of strength she typically exudes. Witnessing her vulnerability, I'm overcome with the realisation of the profound impact of her past on her present.

"Even after discovering that he was part of their malicious plan, I pleaded with him to leave that life behind and strive for a normal life together. To my surprise, he seemed shocked that I still harboured dreams of a regular life. Despite everything, I forgave him once again. He meant everything to me, and all I desired was a life with him. But there's a limit to forgiveness. When I caught him trapping another girl, I was consumed by rage. I attacked him with all my strength, fueled by a desire to see him pay for his actions. He managed to escape and disappeared without a trace.

Unfortunately, I realised that I could never truly escape the kind of life he had gifted me, thanks to the internet, which made the world a global village.

Victims like me become more infamous than the perpetrators. People recognised me everywhere in Bengaluru. I don't blame society for the labels they put on me; I blame myself for falling into his traps."

I try to process the depth of Kalyani's pain and the complexities of her emotions. "How could you endure so much pain and suffering and yet let him go free? What quells your anger towards him? He doesn't deserve your forgiveness," I express my opinion, unable to contain my disbelief at her capacity for forgiveness.

"I don't forgive him, nor do I forgive myself," Kalyani admits, her voice tinged with bitterness. "After he left me, I spiralled out of control. I wandered aimlessly, begged his friends for any information about him, and even contemplated submitting to them if it meant finding him. It took me many months to come to terms with the idea that I had to move forward on my own.

Eventually, I channelled all my emotions into insurmountable hatred, and I resumed my search for him, seeking revenge for the suffering he caused. Hatred became my most powerful and silent drug. It drew me deeper into the world of sex work, where I began earning more and more money. I buried my pain beneath the luxuries that money and clients provided. I even turned to drugs to escape reality and embrace the surreal world that had enveloped me."

"Oh my god! How did you manage to come back to a normal life after all that?" I exclaim in awe.

"Everything has an end; even suffering is not exempt from that," Kalyani replies calmly. "During a raid on a hotel in Bengaluru, I was arrested by the police and sent to a rehabilitation centre due to my powerful intoxication at the time. The investigating officer (CI) was Mr. Bhasker, whom I told you about when we first met in your flat. He played a pivotal role in helping me escape hell. He guided me towards normalising my life. Since leaving the facility, I haven't returned to prostitution but instead work as an informant for the police, living in hiding."

"And what about your hatred?" I ask, curious about her journey towards healing.

"Every emotion, whether positive or negative, has a profound effect on the mind," she explains. "I no longer allow others to occupy my thoughts, and I've come to understand the importance of standing by myself." Her words carry a sense of resilience and self-discovery, illuminating her path from darkness to redemption.

"You are truly remarkable," I salute Kalyani. "Finding your true self after enduring such turmoil in life is astonishingly inspiring. I wish I had the strength to empower myself."

"Everyone has that strength within them, even you," Kalyani reassures me. "You can begin to unleash it the moment you realise it exists within you. Let's grab something to eat over there. I'm terribly hungry." She points towards a bamboo chicken stall nestled on the edge of the parking lot and drives us over to it. I find myself admiring her every move after hearing her story.

As we dine, savouring the flavours of bamboo chicken against the backdrop of mountain winds and the exotic valley view, I receive a call from Karthik, my colleague and friend. He reminds me to check my emails since I've been away from my usual routine for the past week. It dawns on me that I've neglected to check my email amidst recent revelations. Opening the Gmail app, my thoughts involuntarily drift towards the hope of a reply from Saira. Among a few unread work emails, there is nothing from her. Frustrated with my own mind, I reaffirm my commitment to steer my thoughts consciously towards what truly matters, without being swayed by lingering emotions from the past. I realise that the mind must be guided carefully to avoid venturing into forbidden territories.

To get to the actual content of the office emails, I have discovered that I am no longer on the bench and am instructed to report to the manager at the Bengaluru office immediately. Despite being three days late, I feel no sense of urgency. After finishing reading all the emails, I close my mobile and return to my meal.

Kalyani notices my distraction and asks what the office call was about.

"It's from the office. They want me to come back and report to the manager immediately. They say I'm part of a newly formed project team," I explain.

"That's great news! Why don't you hurry up then? When are you leaving?" Kalyani inquires enthusiastically.

"I don't think I will," I respond, surprising her.

"What do you mean? Have you been captivated by the luxuries of a carefree life? Don't get carried away, because you have so much purpose to fulfil in life," Kalyani cautions.

"I'm not being swayed by distractions, but I want to pause and reflect. That's why I don't feel like rushing back," I clarify.

"Interesting! Please, go on," Kalyani urges.

"Do you remember the young farmer who also works in a bank, whom we gave a lift to the other day?" I ask.

"Yes, I remember," Kalyani replies.

"He injected a sense of purpose into me. He knew the value of his work and its meaning. He helped me understand that life is not just about earning money; it's about creating a meaningful existence. In simple terms, earning money alone doesn't capture the essence of life. The key is to do what you love, and the money will follow. It's a valuable lesson I've been trying to embrace for years, but I struggled to fully accept it due to the fear of losing Saira," I explain.

"Now you're talking," Kalyani responds with understanding.

"Even if I fail a thousand times, I want to be a writer. It's something I feel deep inside. I love it, so I do it. I'm prepared to face any consequences that come my way. I'm reshaping the world around me, seeing it with fresh eyes these days. I may have nothing material right now, but I'm not afraid," I express with conviction.

"Truly brave words and clear thinking," Kalyani responds, acknowledging my determination. "This is courage. It doesn't come from a stockpile of assets or a bank balance. It's not derived from having someone beside you, but from the genuine beliefs within yourself. Courage born from adversity is the true power."

I'm not sure if I truly deserve such high praise, but I relish the inspiring words. Leaning back comfortably in my wooden chair, I raise my head slightly with a sense of majestic confidence.

Blocking my view of the valley on the other side of the mountain, a large SUV jostles through the crowd of tourists in search of a parking space and comes to a halt. Gradually, a family of familiar faces begins to emerge from the vehicle, bringing me back to reality. Two children, their faces glowing beneath long brown burkas, eagerly rush towards the edge of the mountain for a view of the valley. A woman dressed similarly in black tries to catch up with them. Two men, one elderly and the other middle-aged, step out from the front seats, adjusting their long kurtas.

"I know these people. I've never met them, but I've seen them somewhere," I think to myself, my mind racing to place them.

Amidst my contemplation, a beautiful young woman steps out of the car from the other side, without a burkha, and my heart skips a beat—it's Saira.

As my heart races uncontrollably upon seeing Saira, I struggle to maintain composure. I excuse myself, pretending to wash my hands, hoping to regain control. Kalyani finishes her meal and joins me, noticing my sudden change in demeanour. I unintentionally bow my head, a clear sign to Kalyani that something is amiss. My heartbeat intensifies, spiralling out of my control.

Moments ago, I felt as majestic as a victorious king, but now I feel meek and vulnerable. Deep-seated memories stir within me, urging me to steal another glance at Saira. The overwhelming longing for her becomes undeniable, causing beads of sweat to form on my face.

The subtle changes in my expression betray to Kalyani that I've spotted someone I shouldn't have. She follows my gaze and notices Saira, who is enjoying the view of the valley, leaning slightly forward against the steel barricades. Kalyani can't tear her eyes away from Saira's beauty.

"She's stunning. She is a real beauty that deserves such high regard?" Kalyani remarks. "It's no surprise she still holds such sway over you, even after a year apart. But she doesn't seem unhappy at all. She's basking in the warmth of the sun in this chilly atmosphere, cheerful with the kids, and clearly adored by everyone in her family."

"Please, let's leave this place," I plead, overcome with discomfort.

"No, let's wait here. I want to see how she reacts when she sees you. There's always a chance to reconnect at any moment," Kalyani suggests.

"That's exactly what I want to avoid," I respond.

"Why?" Kalyani presses.

"Because had she truly wanted to reconnect, she would have reached out to me by now. The fact that she hasn't means she's moved on. I'm just a passing cloud in her life. Let's leave immediately without causing her any discomfort by lingering around," I insist. "Go start the jeep and wait for me down the road around the bend. I'll join you there."

With a heavy heart, I walk away, head bowed. Initially hesitant, Kalyani swiftly reaches the SUV as I requested. Within moments, I join her in the front seat, and we begin descending the main road, leaving behind the valley and the memories that stirred so much turmoil within me.

Even as we move farther away from her, my heart refuses to settle. The Beast hurtles down the winding ghat road towards Vizag, but my mind remains fixated on memories of her. Everything I see blurs into the background as her image persists, igniting a storm of emotions within me. My mind, in its chaotic state, entertains reckless thoughts of going back and confronting her for leaving me in despair a year ago. However, even amidst this turmoil, I recognise the sheer folly of such ideas. Confronting her would only reopen old wounds and serve no purpose other than causing unnecessary pain.

Noticing my unsettled state of mind, Kalyani pulls over the Beast. She offers me a cigarette this time, which I accept without hesitation. We both light up our cigarettes, and I sink into the seat, lost in my thoughts. Kalyani, perceptive as always, senses my need for silence and lets the quiet envelop us.

As Kalyani enjoys her puffs in a relaxed manner, occasionally glancing at me, I find myself unable to engage in conversation. Normally, I wouldn't miss the opportunity to observe a woman smoking, but my mind is too preoccupied to notice anything around me. Every fibre of my being is urging me to turn back and confront Saira. I fight this urge by recalling her last emails and messages, attempting to anchor myself in reality.

"Should we go back?" Kalyani finally breaks the silence, trying to gauge my inner turmoil. Her question hangs in the air, awaiting my response.

"Of course, no!" I affirm decisively, pushing aside the intrusive thoughts of turning back to confront Saira. However, as I watch Kalyani exhale a puff of smoke, I'm momentarily captivated by the enchanting sight. Yet, the image only serves to summon unwanted memories of Saira back to my mind's eye.

Kalyani, attuned to my shifting expressions, suddenly leans in and kisses me, releasing another puff of smoke as her lips meet mine. At that moment, my mind goes blank, consumed by the desire to savor the embrace. Time seems to stretch on as we share this intimate moment, oblivious to the passing onlookers and the gentle sounds of the nearby stream.

As Kalyani pulls away, her words break through the haze of longing. "You should never let her back into your mind, not even when you see another girl smoking. Don't entertain any other thoughts, my dear!" she advises gently, leaving me to grapple with my lingering desires and the echoes of past romance.

Moments later, Kalyani resumes our journey, leaving me in a state of astonishment. This unexpected display of affection from her prompts me to reflect on certain glimpses of her behaviour during our travels. Though I failed to fully appreciate them at the moment, these instances keep replaying in my mind.

As we approach the city borders, I find myself unable to shake off the enchantment of our kiss. Whether it's the mood of the hour, the surroundings, my mental state, or the lingering scent of smoke from our embrace, my consciousness remains fixated on that moment. The landscape that I vividly remembered from our earlier journey now fails to register in my senses during the return trip.

Lost in introspection, I realise that this journey has been a tumultuous ride of emotions, fueled by unexpected encounters and unresolved feelings. The cityscape gradually envelops us, and I brace myself for whatever awaits beyond its familiar borders.

As Kalyani confidently manoeuvres the Beast through the city streets, I try to take in my surroundings while the reel of our association plays in my mind, starting from our introduction on that rainy night in Bengaluru. A sense of belonging begins to seep through my nerves, not solely due to our recent kiss, but because of the culmination of our experiences together.

"Why didn't I see her as more than just an acquaintance until now?" my thoughts ponder. *"Am I unfairly judging her based on her past? Have my physical desires clouded my perception, causing me to resist forming deeper connections with women? Can a simple kiss really create a lasting attachment? How could such a brief moment overshadow years of romance and intense physical connections with Saira?*

Or perhaps this is just how my story with Saira was meant to conclude?"

Despite the lingering thoughts of Saira, I also find myself anticipating the future with Kalyani, which appears promising and glorious. I recognise that the significance of the kiss extends beyond the physical—it feels like Kalyani has assured me that I'm not destined to navigate this lonely life alone.

"Hurrah! Finally, something has emerged that can overshadow 'Sairaness' in myself," I realise with a mix of relief and excitement. It seems that my aimless search for fulfilment has found an end with Kalyani, who welcomes me into her world with open arms, offering a sense of peace and belonging that I've been seeking.

But Kalyani's demeanour remains unchanged, as if our shared moment had little impact on her. She keeps her focus on the road ahead, her expression serene and composed. When I inquire about our destination, Kalyani responds with a smile that reassures me everything is under control. Being with her feels like the ultimate relaxation, and I settle comfortably in my seat as she drives purposefully, sharing her usual witty observations along the way.

I find myself in high spirits, ready to go wherever Kalyani leads me. Occasionally, I steal glances at her, captivated by her presence and temperament. She notices my introspective mood and prompts me with a smile, inviting me to share my thoughts.

Before long, we arrive at the railway station. It dawns on me that it's time to part ways with Kalyani, whose company I've come to cherish deeply. From a phone call she made earlier, I gather that she's bound for Bengaluru, intending to return the Beast to its owner. We meet the owner in the parking lot, exchanging pleasantries and engaging in delightful small talk before he departs with his vehicle.

As the Beast drives away, leaving us amidst the bustling sea of vehicles, a sense of attachment lingers. *"It's life... Things come, people entice you, and everything finds its way,"* I reflect, my thoughts taking on a philosophical tone. Though it may sound trite, the sentiment rings true, encapsulating the fleeting nature of connections and experiences in our lives.

"It will be on platform number 7, but still an hour before it arrives," Kalyani announces upon returning from checking the display screen.

"Shall we head there now or wait a bit?" I inquire.

"Let's go now. It's best to get moving once we've decided," she replies decisively.

"Alright, let's go," I say, offering to carry her heavy bag. Together, we navigate through the bustling crowd towards the first platform, weaving through passengers heading in the opposite direction. I notice men stealing glances at Kalyani, a testament to her beauty. Earlier, she had changed from a saree into a modern yellow top and black leggings at a restroom along the way to the station. Even in casual attire, she exudes a magnetic charm, drawing unintentional attention with her well-proportioned figure and captivating eyes.

As we ascend the stairs to the first platform, we engage in casual conversation, enjoying the anticipation of our journey.

"What time will you reach Bengaluru?" I inquire as we make our way up the stairs.

"Never, by this train," Kalyani responds cryptically.

"What?" I'm taken aback by her unexpected statement.

"Yes, I'm not going to Bengaluru. I'm headed to Kochi," she clarifies.

"That's shocking. You didn't tell me you're relocating?" I respond, trying to process this sudden revelation.

"I wanted to tell you about this. That's why I'm doing it now," she explains casually, continuing to ascend the stairs with ease while I struggle to keep up, burdened by both her heavy bag and the weight of her announcement.

Reaching the walking aisle on the bridge above the trains, I take a deep sigh, shifting the heavy bag from one shoulder to the other. Below us, the trains rumble along the tracks, a visual reminder of the journey ahead.

"Probably, I might not be seeing you again," Kalyani's subdued tone reaches my ears, the last words barely audible as her throat constricts with emotion.

With my head bowed, I watch two trains speed past each other in opposite directions, a sudden visual metaphor for departure and parting.

Her words echo the sentiments I felt earlier outside the station: "It's life… things come, people entice you, and everything goes its way in the end." But the reality of parting with certain people is not as simple or easy as watching a vehicle disappear into the distance.

"Bhasker sir has arranged a job for me in a wedding planner company. He believes this new environment with strangers will help me erase everything from my past and start afresh," Kalyani explains, her voice carrying a mix of resignation and hope. "Life is easier with strangers who don't judge you based on your past."

Her voice, low in tone, beats against my eardrums and heart with a force that drowns out the surrounding noise. Every word and tonal cue from what might be her last words to me holds my complete attention. I've experienced departures in life before, but now I'm starting to feel a renewed sense of optimism for the future. I thought Kalyani would be a lasting companion in my life, yet she's suddenly leaving, leaving me shaken by this unexpected turn of events.

We're seated on a bench with still half an hour until her train arrives.

"You should have confronted her right there," Kalyani suggests.

"No, I have no regrets about not doing that," I respond firmly.

"Regardless of whatever led to her leaving you, you should give yourself a chance to be happy with her again. You seem to be very forgiving."

"Just like you. That's why I didn't want to trouble her anymore."

"I'm not that forgiving kind. I have punished him. Watch it there on the TV," Kalyani points at a nearby television broadcasting local news. The screen displays footage of an unidentified body discovered a few kilometres north of Araku, a location that triggers a memory for me.

"That's the same spot where we stopped last night in the Beast," I confirm.

"Yes, you're right. I encountered him on his way down to the village just before dawn," Kalyani continues.

"And then? What happened?" I inquire, intrigued by the unfolding story.

"I confronted him with pain and agony. Despite my distress, he remained callous and ruthless, expecting me to succumb to his male chauvinism. Fueled by all the torment he inflicted on me, I unleashed my wrath on his drunken self with a wooden shaft. At first, he resisted, but my determination overpowered him. I inflicted severe blows until the alcohol could no longer numb his pain. Finally, as he pleaded for forgiveness, I remained steadfast in my resolve. With a swift, vehement kick to his abdomen, I sent him tumbling into the valley. I'm certain his body must have been ravaged when discovered," Kalyani recounts with a sense of closure and resolution.

The news presenter's report on the TV sends a chilling shock through me. "Including the head, even other parts remain shattered and unidentifiable," the broadcast describes the gruesome state of the body.

I turn to look at Kalyani, noticing her unusual blinking, perhaps an attempt to manage her emotions. It's not sympathy I see in her eyes, but a sense of fulfillment. Before I can fully process what I've witnessed, she speaks, her voice carrying an air of resolution. "Some animals don't deserve forgiveness. You may have noticed my satisfaction and composure on our return journey. I am indeed redeemed from the guilt of succumbing to him in the past. But as we have reached the station just now, I feel I am still a tormented soul with no possible redemption in this life."

She continues, her words filled with emotion. "At least I can say, as I wholeheartedly call you a saint, that you have unanimously earned my love and admiration. But I can never imagine becoming a stain in your spotless, absolute sainthood. Though it means a mere death to me, I resolve to leave you forever. Shaan! Please leave me here and go."

Her cracking tone resonates deeply, and I see the pain in her eyes. "You know, I couldn't allow myself to stay in an old-age home either. I cannot escape the things I've done in the past. I cannot stay in anyone's life more than this," she confesses, locking eyes with me.

I find myself speechless, with no words left to say. Standing up, I bid her farewell. "Goodbye, Kalyani! I won't stand in your way."

With a heavy heart, I turn away, leaving behind a complex mix of emotions and memories, unsure of what the future holds for either of us. I walk to the end of the platform, my steps wobbling with a mix of vigor, anxiety, and a tumultuous ocean of emotions swirling within. I don't dare look back at Kalyani as I make my way. It's been a long time since I've felt this way, reminiscent of when Saira left me with a note and a phone call. The devastation of reading her final email comes flooding back to me now, a fresh wound on a different chapter of my life.

With each thundering thud of my footsteps, I push forward, the station fading behind me in a blur. I doubt Kalyani is watching; my sole focus is on escaping this overwhelming moment, retreating swiftly from the train station.

*****

Sitting quietly beside my mother on the cot, I observe her composed demeanour as she shares the latest happenings around our home. She speaks of the ongoing struggles with our agricultural work, how it's failing to sustain us, and the pressing need for an alternative source of income. The weight of economic setbacks weighs heavily on her words, reminding me of the two acres of land we lost due to financial difficulties.

Although my mother doesn't explicitly mention it, I can discern the underlying worry in her eyes—the need for more financial support, especially for her health. As she talks, my mind is consumed with various thoughts, but one recurrent realisation stands out: *"Whoever comes close to me eventually leaves, just as Kalyani."*

I find myself grappling with a profound realisation and a stark reality that seem to pull me in opposite directions. On one hand, I'm determined to pursue what brings me joy and fulfilment. Yet, on the other hand, I'm confronted with the practical necessity of securing a job for survival. The question looms large before me: *"Should I prioritise survival or happiness?"*

The dilemma intensifies as I consider the impact on my mother. I cannot find happiness at the expense of her suffering, nor can I continue in a job that feels heartless and devoid of meaning. How can I seek personal satisfaction while knowing that my choices may cause my mother distress?

It's another chilly night, and my mother is in the kitchen, tending to the firewood stove that warms our modest home. She prefers the simple, earthy setting of our kitchen, content with the basics for cooking and living that our surroundings provide. Never once has she asked for comfort or luxury. All her expenditures were directed towards my father's health and my education, with the hope that I would quickly establish myself in life and carry our family forward. It's not her fault that despite her sacrifices, my father passed away, and I have yet to contribute financially.

Earlier today, I met with the man who lent us money on interest, pleading for a six-month extension on repayment. Though initially hesitant, he relented, understanding our shared struggles as neighbours. However, he made it clear that this would be the last extension he could offer, as he, too, is working towards building a home for his own family.

Amidst these pressing realities, I feel compelled to set aside my pursuit of personal fulfilment and return to Bengaluru for the job. The weight of responsibility and the urgency of addressing our family's financial challenges weigh heavily on my mind, pushing me towards practical decisions over personal aspirations.

As I sip my tea, my mother's words resonate deeply within me, the crackling fire casting a warm glow in our kitchen. She's right—it's during our darkest moments, when options seem scarce, that our true strength emerges. Her hands deftly arrange the fire sticks in the mud stove, her actions mirroring the resilience she embodies.

"Let your decision be free from the weight of my health or our home's problems," she advises, her voice steady and wise. "In five years from now, I want you to look back without regrets. Clarify your priorities and choose wisely. If you believe in your abilities, you can brave any risk to pursue your dreams."

My mother's unwavering support has never made me feel small or timid, even amid our family's challenges. She embodies the strength of a resilient mother, instilling in me the belief that one must confront and challenge life's obstacles. "Life is filled with problems," she continues, her voice filled with conviction. "What matters is choosing the path that leads to a better, more fulfilling life. No one promises a life without challenges, but it's how we face them that defines us."

Reflecting on my past attempts to showcase my writing skills, I recall sending drafts of technical articles to Nithya, a freelance writer and editor in Bengaluru. Her feedback was not encouraging—she pointed out that my tone was didactic, and the articles lacked depth and informativeness. Despite believing in my abilities, I feel disheartened by my inability to impress her. It leaves me questioning my skills and abilities.

As I grapple with these thoughts, memories of Kalyani and Saira resurface, serving as poignant reminders of my struggles to retain meaningful connections. Saira's abrupt departure, akin to discarding a useless rag, still lingers, undermining my confidence and affecting my decision-making.

"I should never let her into my mind again," my thoughts continue to churn. *"Maybe it's necessary to hold some level of resentment towards those who discard us. Excessive forgiveness can be mistaken for weakness. Just because I don't blame her doesn't mean I should suffer for my own mistakes. I need to banish her from my foolish brain. In that case, I no longer require anyone else to move on in my life. Kalyani's departure succinctly teaches me that one must take charge of their own life. Life is about striving in solitude, not falling into loneliness."*

Reflecting on the torment Kalyani endured from her lover, yet continued to trust him, I marvel at her resilience. It took her years to see his true nature, and more years to exact revenge for her suffering. Despite the turmoil eating away at her from within, she never appeared to burn out. She faced each challenge with a smile, fueled by the hatred she harbored for him.

In the months since Saira left, I've begun to explore the reasons behind her abrupt departure from my life. Perhaps she was propelled by some measure of resentment and discontent. Love alone, without any negativity, may not be sufficient. I've come to realise that even negative emotions have their importance. Without experiencing hell, paradise holds little value.

The next day, I am drafting a letter to Nithya. The other day, when I wanted to delete all contacts related to Saira, I almost deleted Nithya's contact as well, since she was introduced to me by Saira. However, considering the importance of our connection for my creative journey, I decided against removing her from my contact list.

"Dear Nithya,

Each time I sent you my drafts, you pointed out that my self was missing in my writing. I struggled hard to understand what it meant. Though I tried several times to infuse my voice into the articles, it felt forced and artificial. It didn't resonate with the real me. Finally, I realised that all this time I've been approaching writing from the wrong angle—trying to create something that doesn't truly reflect who I am.

Yesterday, I took some time to reflect on myself, and I found the true expression of my thoughts in my diary. Admittedly, I wrote it as a way to address my feelings towards Saira, especially after she left me. The longing, the pain of missing her, and the sense of living in her universe even after she was gone—these themes are prominently featured in my diary. Additionally, there are two other important characters who significantly influenced my thoughts and experiences.

I believe that this personal journey and the characters involved would make for an engaging story in my novel. Today, I'll start typing it out on my iPad and aim to send it to you within a month. I'm hopeful that it will turn out to be an interesting and authentic piece."

I meticulously review the letter multiple times before hitting send to Nithya. At first, I had doubts about whether the concept would capture interest, but I've come to believe that detailing every significant scene between Saira and me could be compelling. By incorporating Vishwa and Kalyani into the narrative, I aim to create a story that resonates deeply with readers, allowing them to see parallels in their own lives. Ultimately, I hope that this story will convey a positive message about resilience in the face of romantic disappointment and life's challenges, inspiring readers to navigate their own struggles with optimism and determination.

Chapter 9: Catharsis

"The deeper your love, the greater your anguish;
In prolonged suffering, life loses its lustre;
Yet from darkness, the soul finds strength anew;
The brighter the soul, the loftier writing flourishes;
With each word penned, you delve deeper into self;
The further you excavate, the mightier she looms up."

The next morning, I find myself sitting on the bed, my fingers dancing across the keys of my iPad. It's 6 am, and I've been at this for the past two hours. Instead of directly copying from my diary, I'm using it as a wellspring of past incidents. Throughout the night, my thoughts refused to let me sleep, weaving the story in the recesses of my mind. By the time I finally rose at 4 am, I had a clear idea of where to begin. Now, two hours into my writing session, the words on the screen seem scant. Each incident from the diary transports me back to those days with her, pulling me deeper into the scenes and momentarily obstructing my writing process. Yet, the mere act of persistently typing, without pause or screen closure, motivates me to continue. The narrative unfolds gradually as I relive each moment, feeling the story come alive with every keystroke. My determination to capture these memories in vivid detail propels me forward, despite the challenges that arise along the way.

In the afternoon, I find myself grappling with an intense desire to sift through our collection of photos. The photos hold the potential to clarify specific details crucial for certain scenes, ensuring consistency in my narrative. However, a voice of caution within me warns against opening her file, fearing it might disrupt the tranquil, creative process I've carefully nurtured. I decide to take a break for lunch, hoping the respite will bring clarity to my decision-making. I am mindful of the potential hurdles that revisiting the past may pose to my writing flow. The emotional weight of confronting these memories is palpable; it's excruciating to delve into what troubles me the most. Initially confident in the wealth of material for a captivating story, I now confront my hesitance to draw directly from the deepest wellsprings of experience. This acknowledgement weighs heavily upon me as I strive to strike a delicate balance between artistic expression and emotional vulnerability in my storytelling journey.

By evening, I come to a stark realisation of my exhaustion, both physically and emotionally, as I find myself slipping into involuntary sleep multiple times over the past hour. It dawns on me that I've been drained by various demands in recent days, leaving my mind craving much-needed relaxation. This pattern of drifting off when trying to focus on something is reminiscent of my experiences with reading after a long hiatus. When reading isn't a regular habit, the mind must push through this initial foggy, sleepy phase to reach the bright clarity of immersive reading. Similarly, I find that writing follows a parallel course. Despite these brief periods of rest, I persist in my writing efforts, pushing through to continue deep contemplation and capture fleeting thoughts in written form. This dedication mirrors the journey of engaging with a text after a spell of absence—each effort propelling me towards a clearer, more focused state of creative expression.

As evening descends, the short winter days quickly surrender to longer periods of darkness in this region. By the time dusk settles in, I find myself once again surrounded by her presence in every direction. Saira, whom I've been unable to shake from my thoughts since last night, looms larger than ever in my mind after a prolonged absence. Despite encountering various people and places in recent days that I thought might distract or overlap with her memory, reading through the diary acts as a gateway back to the indelible past.

The moments recorded in the diary are merely the visible peaks of a vast submerged mountain, gradually unfurling my mind to roam freely through the many facets of my life during those days. After an extended period, I begin to feel the inevitable pull to revisit her photos, to reach out with a call or message, or to somehow reconnect with her. As I delve deeper into the memoirs of our love story, I find myself typing with blurred vision, my eyes moist with emotion, unable to escape the overwhelming nostalgia and longing that accompany these cherished memories. Each word typed becomes a testament to the enduring impact she had on my life and the complex emotions that still linger beneath the surface.

As I immerse myself deeper in the written memoirs, I sternly admonish my weaker self to steel against the emotions that threaten to overwhelm. Each moment captured within these pages feels like a profound intervention in my life, as if orchestrated by some celestial force. Saira, whom I have always held in the highest regard, akin to a divine being, occupies my thoughts relentlessly.

My thoughts ponder, *"No matter how hard I try, I cannot identify a single reason that would justify forgetting her. My mind seems adept at recalling every kindness she bestowed upon me while conveniently disregarding my own acts of devotion towards her. This selective memory became apparent during our last conversation when she asked what I had done for her, leaving me unable to respond. It wasn't for lack of examples, but rather a reluctance to quantify my feelings into tangible actions. This hesitation, I grasp, stems from the depth of my unparalleled love for her. I firmly believe that true love should not require keeping score or proving oneself through deeds. If I must catalogue my actions to validate my love, then it ceases to be genuine. Love, to me, is not about proving oneself; it transcends the need for validation or recognition. I harbor no desire to convince anyone, not even her, of the intensity, purity, and divine nature of my emotions. My love endures independent of external validation, cherished for its sincerity and sacredness known only to me."*

As night falls, her presence haunts me relentlessly, leaving me at a crossroads with no clear path forward. If I choose to continue on this journey, delving even deeper into my memories with her, I know I will have to face intense suffering. Yet, if I decide to give up now, I see no other viable direction to take. Writing is my refuge, a means of confronting and processing these emotions, even if it means confronting painful memories. Despite the anguish it brings, I cannot forsake this outlet that allows me to navigate the complexities of my emotions and experiences.

I recognise that overcoming this obstacle in my writing requires restraining my hands from reaching for her photos on my phone, averting my eyes from reminders of her presence everywhere, resisting the allure of our intimate memories in my mind, and preventing my heart from entertaining thoughts of reconnecting with her. Despite the pain inflicted by these self-imposed limitations, I press onward on my path, knowing that confronting these challenges will ultimately pave the way for a brighter future self. Each step forward feels like navigating through a barrage of pointed and self-created obstacles from my past, but I remain steadfast in my pursuit of personal growth and creative resilience.

Last night, I was filled with unflagging confidence in my story and my abilities. However, within a day, everything has shifted. I now find myself uncertain about continuing the narrative, overwhelmed by memories of her that resurfaced during the writing process. Yet, I cannot simply abandon the story, accepting the harsh reality of my life without her. Despite my efforts, I manage to complete just the fifth page of the document, with more than three pages dedicated to justifying my actions to my inner self for losing her.

Two conflicting emotions tug at my mind relentlessly. On one side, I am consumed by self-blame for what transpired between us. On the other hand, I wrestle with the fear of losing myself entirely in pursuit of my writing. I know all too well that once I lose touch with my true self, I will struggle to compose even a single sentence.

Surrounded by internal barriers, I shut my iPad and set it aside, stepping outside into the night with an acute numbness engulfing my mind and body. Despite the discomfort, I cling to a glimmer of hope that the cold of the night might bring clarity and calmness, allowing me to resume my writing with renewed vigour tomorrow.

In the morning, I am on our farm with my mother. Last night, I asked her to wake me early so I could start writing at the crack of dawn, a time I deemed divine for creativity. However, upon awakening, my initial thoughts were far from promising. Instead of succumbing to negativity, I decided to head to our paddy field at dawn. I believed that by engaging in a different activity, I could allow my brain to shift gears and redirect its thinking. Creative writing is not unfamiliar territory for me, yet while I encounter challenges, they stem from within rather than from the act of writing itself.

I find myself constantly surrounded by memories of Saira, reminiscent of the initial months after her departure. Revisiting our past together has profoundly impacted my daily life, fueling a growing urge to reach out to her again with each passing moment. As a precaution, I deliberately left my mobile phone at home to prevent impulsive actions driven by these emotions, granting myself time to reflect and regain composure.

Amidst this internal struggle, I immerse myself in field work until well past noon, a welcome deviation from my thoughts. When the session concludes, my mother announces it's time to return home, marking the end of our tasks for the day.

In the evening, I engage in conversation with my mother, discussing her health and medications. Later, in the late evening hours, I have made a significant decision by sending my resignation letter to my manager. Despite feeling physically and emotionally drained, my determination to pursue writing remains steadfast. I refuse to play it safe or entertain fallback options in case of failure. This act of decisive action reinforces my courage, and I settle on the cot with my iPad, opening the document for my writing.

I am resolute in allowing Saira's memories to impact me deeply, yet I am equally determined to maintain control over my impulses. I am committed to navigating through these poignant memories and continuing with my writing, undeterred by the challenges and emotions they may bring forth.

The narration goes like this on my iPad. *"The darkness outside seems to fade away in comparison to the light that radiates within me, fueled by your presence in my heart. This light was first kindled on the day we crossed paths at the college technical fest. I remember vividly the moment you descended into the auditorium, dressed in a stunning gold and maroon long top, a captivating sight amid the bustling event. Meanwhile, I stood by the stage, eager to participate, but faced rejection due to the repetitive nature of my chosen topic. As I lingered there, hoping for a breakthrough, you unexpectedly made your entrance from the highest rows of seats, almost like a celestial arrival.*

My heart skipped a beat at the sight of you, though my mind was still preoccupied with the desire to make an impact at the fest. You engaged in conversations with fellow students and lecturers, your expression clouded with disappointment. Eventually, you made your way towards the stage, a sense of hopelessness etched on your features. At that instant, a surge of courage propelled me forward, drawing me irresistibly towards you. I found myself compelled to inquire about your troubles, and when our eyes met, you glanced at me with a reckless abandon that momentarily transfixed me."

Surrounded by overwhelming negativity, I deliberately chose to immerse myself in our brightest memory—our first meeting. As I began to write about that cherished moment, a sense of calm washed over me, and I could vividly feel her light still glowing within my heart. Describing her as gloriously as I perceived her that day, my words flowed onto the page, albeit with tears welling in my eyes. If given the opportunity to turn back time, I would eagerly relive that unforgettable day in the auditorium when our paths first crossed. It seems I have almost failed to identify that I am addressing her directly, which should not be the case pertaining to the novel.

Despite the passing night, the scene I am recounting seems to stretch endlessly, revealing the depth and significance of that singular encounter. An hour of intensive writing envisages that I could easily create a voluminous book centered solely around this particular scene—starting from the moment we were introduced as strangers to the warm, enjoyable conversation that marked the end of the day, with each detail etched vividly in my memory and now on the pages before me.

For the first time, I find immense joy in the act of writing, and I attribute this newfound passion to her presence within the scene. With each paragraph I write, I feel a longing for the story to never reach its conclusion, only to be reminded with a bitter laugh that this tale had already concluded a year ago. This moment of insanity elicits a few more tears trickling down my cheeks. In an effort to distance myself from her memory, I intentionally shift my focus to a sombre scene from the next chapter where loneliness reigns supreme.

Over the course of these months, I've come to realise the danger of glorifying someone who will never return to my life—it can disrupt my peace of mind. Despite this, I acknowledge that harbouring hatred toward her is impossible for me. My emotions are complex, entangled with love, longing, and a sense of resignation to the reality of our parting.

After completing the scene within the hour, I feel emotionally exhausted. The process has taken a toll on me, leaving me drained for the rest of the day. Setting aside the iPad, I collapse onto my bed. The weight of emotions and memories lingers, but for now, I surrender to the need for rest and recuperation.

*****

It has been ten days since I embarked on the journey of writing my novel. Throughout this time, while the external world remained quiet, my internal landscape was tumultuous and intense. To maintain my focus and emotional balance, I adopted a method of alternating between writing loving scenes and depicting sad experiences one after the other. This approach helped prevent me from spiralling into despair or disrupting her peaceful and happy life.

Despite facing relentless hallucinations and overwhelming urges to reach out to her, I remained steadfast in my mission to complete each chapter methodically. I felt a profound sense of accomplishment upon finishing the first four chapters of my novel. I navigated this creative endeavor without any external guides, relying solely on my instincts and emotions to guide me.

By interweaving scenes from our love story with the painful experiences I endured after her departure, the narrative of my novel is taking shape remarkably well. Each word penned serves as a cathartic release, transforming my inner turmoil into a compelling story that reflects both love and loss, hope and heartache.

As I reach the halfway point of my novel, a clear picture of the story unfolds in my mind. I am conscious of not overwhelming readers with the highest emotional peaks of the life I am depicting. Instead, I aim to guide them towards understanding the pathways out of the web of negativity that circumstances can create. Although I continue to suffer, a burden I may carry for a lifetime, I strive to convey a sense of resilience and possibility through my writing. Writing has become my steadfast companion on this journey, an effective tool in navigating the depths of my buried memories without succumbing to self-destruction. Surrounded by the turbulent waves of emotions, I find solace in the act of writing, holding onto this lifeline as I chart a course towards healing and acceptance.

As new characters enter my story, my writing process becomes more fluid and engaging. However, amidst this creative flow, I am confronted with the challenge of my mother's ill health. I find myself spending numerous hours in hospital waiting rooms, with my iPad on my lap, determined to continue typing and immersing myself in my fictional world despite the disruptions of the real-life surroundings. In the midst of this, I have reached a state where I lose track of time and the natural shifts of day and night, deeply absorbed in portraying my story against all odds.

In this process, I am reminded of the teachings of sages who emphasise the importance of flow and focus in our work. For the first time, I am experiencing this concept firsthand. The depth of my engagement and immersion in my writing illustrates the potential success of my novel. As I become naturally drawn into my work, I am convinced that the results will reflect this organic commitment and dedication. The more effortlessly and authentically we are able to immerse ourselves in our creative endeavours, the greater the potential for a meaningful and impactful outcome.

In just two months, I've completed my first draft and immediately delved into the editing process. Alongside this, I've crafted a three-page synopsis of the story, ready to be shared with editors like Nithya and others for their invaluable feedback. However, this step has brought forth numerous emotional hurdles, as revisiting my work requires reliving the moments captured within the story. It's a bittersweet realisation that I am now missing those wonderful and glorious moments that once defined my life with her. This awakening weighs heavily on me, reinforcing the belief that I am incomplete without her presence. Yet, despite this emotional turmoil, I am compelled to continue with my work.

With tear-filled eyes, a heavy heart, and an outwardly artificial smile for others, I press forward. Through this process, I begin to understand the true essence of life—it's not always about what happens or what we hope will happen; rather, it's about embracing the present moment, however challenging or painful it may be. I consider myself blessed to have experienced countless lovely moments with her over the span of six years, each cherished memory holding immeasurable value in my heart. The joy I feel, even through tears, when reminiscing about those moments is profound.

I've come to acknowledge that I may never fully move on from her, but I can choose to live within the happiness of her aura for the rest of my life. I release myself from judgment and self-blame, acknowledging that she remains with me always, without remorse or resentment. This acceptance brings a sense of peace and allows me to navigate life's journey with a newfound perspective rooted in love and gratitude.

Two days after sending the synopsis to Nithya, I received a reply email filled with her overwhelming response to the depiction of pure love in my story and the depth of the characters I've created. She acknowledges that I have skillfully avoided making the story one-sided by focusing on my own narrative and experiences without delving into our shared history. Nithya appreciates my approach of not assigning blame or resentment towards her for my struggles and suffering, recognising the complexity and maturity in my storytelling.

Furthermore, she praises my decision to leave the reasons for our breakup ambiguous within the narrative, noting that this choice adds a layer of intrigue and universality to the story. We both agree that sometimes, when parting ways becomes inevitable, the specific reasons behind it become secondary to the emotional impact and aftermath.

Receiving Nithya's positive email fills me with elation, marking the first time I've received such encouraging feedback from her. Her response aligns perfectly with the kind of reception I had hoped for when I first embarked on this writing journey. It's a wonderful moment that inevitably brings me back to memories of Saira. She always believed in my skills but doubted my dedication to completing a book on my own.

At this moment, there's a strong urge to share my entire manuscript with Saira—not to impress her, but as a heartfelt offering. She has always been the light that illuminates my soul, and now, the pages of my novel. Yet, despite this longing, I resist the temptation to reach out to her. I recognise that I don't want to disrupt her life in any way, as has always been my decision.

My nights are often consumed by thoughts of her or dreams where she returns to me. Many times, I've awakened with a sense of fleeting joy, only to be harshly reminded of the reality of her absence. Tonight is no different; I lie awake, wrestling with the desire to reach out to her. Despite these impulses, I maintain control over my emotions and resist the urge to contact her.

Suddenly, a notification from Gmail interrupts my thoughts. As I pick up my phone, I am stunned to see an email from Saira, indicated by her familiar greetings in the notification. My heart races with anticipation and uncertainty as I open the app, eager to read her words after so many days of silence. My mind races with wild possibilities, imagining scenarios where she wants to reconcile and be with me again.

"Hi, I hope *your* doing well." (her usual mistake in writing). "I think you need to find some other story rather than involving me in it. Though you changed my name in the novel, it will become a testimony among my friends and acquaintances to prove what happened between us. It might eventually become the greatest hurdle to my peaceful life further.

Please understand my concern and remove my part from the book.

I wish you good luck."

As I read Saira's email repeatedly, my heart continues to race uncontrollably. Despite the cold winter, my eyes begin to perspire with nervousness. Suppressing the immediate urge to reply to her message, I decide to leave my bed and step away from the iPad. *"I might be tempted to respond hastily if I stay here,"* I think to myself.

Leaving the room, I step outside into the wide expanse of cold darkness. The chilly air surrounds me, providing a stark contrast to the turmoil within. I find myself drawn to the mud stove located nearby, still emitting a small flame that seems on the verge of extinguishing. Sitting before the stove, I am enveloped in its warmth and the flickering light of the fire.

Alone with my thoughts, I gaze into the flames, contemplating deeply. Fire has long been believed to possess the power to purify and cleanse. As I add more wood to it, I allow myself to introspect, seeking clarity amongst the swirling emotions and desires that Saira's unexpected email has stirred within me.

As I continue to fixate on the fire, monumental moments from ages past are stirred within me, engraved deep within my buried soul. Minutes pass by, my gaze unwavering as I remain transfixed by the core of the flames. Almost instinctively, my hands supply firewood as needed, seamlessly tending to the blaze without conscious effort.

Amid this intimate communion with the fire, the world around me undergoes a magical transformation. Suddenly, I find myself transported to a cold beach, the only warmth emanating from the fireplace in front of me. A chilling breeze sweeps through the air, enveloping me in its icy embrace. Despite the cold, the heat from the fire begins to spread throughout my body, gradually thawing the chill of the surrounding air.

In this surreal moment, I find myself transported back to a cherished memory—a memory of myself and Saira nestled in a tent facing a campfire on Paradise Beach in Pondicherry. The image emerges effortlessly from the depths of my consciousness, a testament to the enduring power of our shared experiences. I recall with clarity the fervent plea I made to the local youth to arrange the romantic setup—a tent facing the campfire and the sea. It was Saira's dream to stay in such a setting, and I was determined to make it a reality.

With the help of the locals, I arranged every detail, ensuring that our night on the beach was nothing short of magical. As we camped in the tent, surrounded by the warmth of the blazing fire and the soothing sounds of the sea, I knew that it was a moment we would cherish forever—a moment of pure joy and connection encompassed by the beauty of nature.

In the warmth of the flames, there is no room for anything to come between our naked selves cuddled up under the blanket, as if the fire itself is a testament to our unbreakable connection. However, the chill at my back serves as a poignant reminder of a whispered confession from Saira during one of our intimate encounters. In a moment of ecstatic passion, she revealed, "Your body feels so cold, yet it quenches my rising desires. My relative warmth perfectly complements your passionate needs. You are the missing piece that completes me, and I become your most fervent longing. Our union is the harmonious merging of two halves of a single entity."

She pressed her lips against mine, the warmth of her breath mingling with mine, as if to merge our very essence into one. With each tender touch of her lips, she whispered words that resonated deep within my soul. "Do we need this breathing at all, my love?" she murmured, her voice trembling with emotion. "When we have each other, time seems to stand still. In these moments, when we are fully open and vulnerable, our connection is all that matters. Your touch sustains me, your breath gives me life."

In the intimacy of the tent, surrounded only by the vastness of nature, there was no fear, no hesitation—only a profound desire to be together. We were not intoxicated by alcohol, but rather by the elixir of love, which enveloped us in its embrace and rendered us breathless with its intensity.

As she spoke, her voice soft and inviting, she asked, "Do you want a smoke now?" My response was firm, "No, nothing else between us." With that, we surrendered ourselves to a long, passionate embrace, losing track of time as our lips met in a fervent kiss. At that moment, she was all-consuming, yet I felt as if I were soaring among the stars in the vast expanse of the cosmos.

When she finally pulled away, her eyes sparkled with a childlike innocence as she posed the question that always left me speechless, "Shaanu! How much do you love me?" The sweetness of her tone still reverberates in me. It was a question she asked whenever she was overcome with ecstasy, and for which I could never provide a satisfactory answer. Each time she asked, I found myself pondering the immeasurable depths of love, wondering if such a thing could ever be quantified.

With a helpless smile, I awaited her response, knowing that she would answer her own question in countless ways. This time, I hoped for a new insight, a fresh perspective that would illuminate the complexities of our bond.

"In your hands, Shaanu, resides the entirety of my being. No distance or circumstance can keep us apart. I've willingly surrendered all of myself to you, granting you entrance into every corner of my heart without reservation. There's no secret, no hidden chamber that you cannot explore, for you possess the key to every part of me. You are my boundless love, my eternal muse, and in your embrace, I find complete ecstasy," she declared, her words carrying a weight of sincerity and vulnerability.

"Do you know why I never ask you to delete my private and self-shot videos that I sent you?" she continued, her gaze intent. "I know you would not watch them again and again because I am there right in front of you to do whatever you desire. Yet, I kept recording our romantic rendezvous, particularly on your phone. It's not just because my phone is inspected by my family when I go home. I am not drunk now, and I tell you this with all my senses, remember!"

With each word, her sincerity pierced through the air, leaving an indelible mark on my heart. "Even by using those videos, you please wake me up from a deadly sleep of departed life from you. Use them to get me back to you from any kind of unfathomable situation we might be in in the future. I grant you all the rights on our personal videos and pictures to bail me out of a life without you at any juncture. Even after years of separation due to my foolish thinking, please pull me back toward you by all means. Or else, remember Shaanu, it will be hell for me."

As she finished speaking, a few drops of her tears showered on my face, carrying the weight of her emotions and the depth of her love.

As the most powerful snippet of memory pierces me like a sharp arrow to the heart, I find myself face to face with my own naked self, illuminated by the flickering flames of the fire. His gaze penetrates deep into my soul, urging me to take action to reunite him with his eternal companion. With a silent intensity, his eyes speak volumes, conveying the profound longing for union with his beloved.

At this juncture, as I confront my own naked truth, I am compelled to confront the depths of my own desires and the barriers that stand in the way of true connection. His silent plea resonates within me, stirring something primal and profound—a yearning for wholeness and completion that transcends the bounds of time and space.

"My Saira is always prepared to do whatever it takes to reach me. She has provided everything necessary to rescue her from her miserable life. All she desires is me. The smile and happiness she displays in front of her family do not reflect her true self. As the only person in the world who truly understands her, she must be eagerly awaiting an opportunity to contact me or find me, even if it means resorting to less than honourable methods. At this very moment, she may be pondering what is preventing me from using the most powerful tool to draw her closer to me. Frustrated by my indecision, she may be wandering in this region, searching for me everywhere. I know that she has always loved beaches and the southern part of the country. She has never been fond of visiting hill stations or mountainous regions. So, what else could be the reason for her to travel to my location with her family?"

Staring at my naked self, unblinking and unwavering, has a profound effect that brings tears streaming down my cheeks. Perhaps it's just a speck of ash lifted from the fire that adds to the moisture in my eyes. However, the true reason for my tears seems to be my inability to answer my naked self. Yet, he persists, undeterred by my emotional turmoil.

"Saira has been my companion for ages, our bond transcending mere lifetimes. Our souls are destined to unite in each incarnation, yearning for each other and finding solace in our sublime union. Across countless lifetimes, our divine connection remains unbreakable, unaffected by the mere passage of a year. She holds the elixir for all the ailments of my soul, a truth proven time and again in our previous births.

In one lifetime, her eternal kiss saved my desolate soul from wandering in the desert. In another, she guided me when I was adrift in the vast ocean. And in this life, she has been my steadfast companion in navigating the jungle of self-created fears and worries. The only step required of me is to use the key to unlock the gates of happiness and return to her embrace.

I do not doubt that she might question me for using our intimate photos and videos. To dispel any lingering doubts in my mind, I intend to send her a snapshot of our deep kiss via email. No words are necessary in the message; the picture speaks volumes. Sending her this image will certainly break down all barriers, prompting her to contact me by any means necessary. It's the message she's been waiting for months—a test of my commitment to winning her back. Her perennial question during our relationship, "How much do you love me?" finds its answer now. I'm willing to go to any lengths to ensure our reunion, to fulfil the destiny of our souls entwined over countless lifetimes. So, I'll answer her question by sending our kissing photo. If there's no response, then there's no question of it. Go retrieve my mobile, open the repository of our love stored in its images and videos, and select the best one to welcome her back. Our true selves reside there, in the personal folder—where Saira and I exist in the purest form of love."

In a trance-like state, I rise from my seat without conscious awareness of my surroundings. It feels as though my mind and body are being directed by an external force, leaving me unable to resist. With a sense of detachment, I retrieve my mobile and diary and make my way to the fireplace, guided solely by the mysterious compulsion. Sitting cross-legged on the ground, I place the diary beside me and open my mobile. Navigating with an eerie detachment, I open the personal folder, a repository of cherished memories with Saira. It's a surreal experience to revisit this space after a year, almost as if I'm caught between reality and a dream.

The naked self of mine lifts his chin up slightly, as if urging me to proceed. With a plethora of thumbnails displaying her face, my soul begins to stir with newfound energy. Across from me, the wild figure offers a faint smile, his eyes wide open with anticipation. Slowly, I extend my index finger to select one of the pictures and begin to scroll upward. With each line of thumbnails that passes, a wave of emotion washes over me, and the naked self's eyes seem to glow even brighter, as if poised to ignite millions of sparks within my soul.

As I navigate through the thumbnails, they seem to beckon, eager to reveal themselves. The cascade of images and video clips scrolling up feels like a heavyweight pressing on my chest, matching the frantic rhythm of my heartbeats. The naked self staring at me nods repeatedly in wild anticipation, longing for release from eternal loneliness. With each image waiting to be opened, I feel a surge of emotions building up within me. The mere act of selecting any image from the multitude before my eyes threatens to unleash a tsunami of feelings, overpowering and uncontrollable. Every cell in my body feels electrified, poised to experience a celestial moment of redemption for my devastated soul.

My arm feels heavy with emotion, immobilised by the flood of feelings washing over me. Tears blur my vision, making it difficult to bear the overwhelming surge of devotion. Meanwhile, my naked self moves his hands in a rhythmic pattern, dancing with anticipation. With great effort, I manage to place my finger on the corner of the screen, wiping away tears to clear my vision. In a decisive moment, I select "select all" and press the delete button without hesitation.

The action sends a profound wave coursing through my body, from my head down my spine, awakening senses I never knew existed. Instantly, the mobile slips from my grasp, tumbling to the ground. As I wipe tears from my cheeks and glance around, I realise the naked self has vanished. With newfound determination, I retrieve the mobile and proceed to delete the personal folder from the recycle bin as well. A sense of positivity washes over my soul as I open my contacts and start deleting all numbers associated with her. In the blink of an eye, my inner world undergoes a drastic transformation.

With a heavy heart, I scroll through my general gallery, meticulously searching for any traces of her intertwined among the myriad of images. Each photo holds a memory, a moment shared, but now they serve as painful reminders of what once was. Slowly, deliberately, I select each one, feeling the weight of my actions with each press of the delete button. As I watch the images vanish from my screen, consumed by the digital void, I feel a sense of liberation mingled with sorrow.

As I navigate through the apps on my phone, my fingers trembling slightly, I find her chatting on WhatsApp. Each message contains a piece of our shared history, from our first interactions to our final goodbyes. Deleting the whole chat page feels like erasing a part of myself, but I know it's necessary for her peace of mind. With a heavy heart, I press the delete button, feeling the weight of each deleted message as if it were a piece of my soul.

With determination coursing through my veins, I clutch the diary containing the source of my novel. Tear by tear, I rip its pages and cast them into the fire. Months ago, when experts advised me to take this step to break free from her hold, I couldn't bring myself to do it. I couldn't bear to burn her memories for my own sake. But now, as I contemplate the possibility that these memories might be causing her distress, I act swiftly. I refuse to allow even the slightest chance of her suffering because of me.

Tearing five or six pages at a time, I crush them in my hand before tossing them into the flames. Each page that meets the fire feels like a sacrifice, a small offering for her happiness. The thought of her wanting her part removed from the novel sends a chill down my spine. If she no longer finds solace in the words I've written, then the book itself is dead to me. My first book, destined for a premature death before it's ever read by another soul. As the last of the diary's pages turn to ash, I sit by the fire, a silent witness to the destruction of my creation. Despite the flames raging before me, my eyes betray me, spilling forth a stream of hopeless emotion. Alone with my thoughts, I have nothing left to say, nothing left to write, and no glimmer of hope to guide me.

"Now, I believe, I have precisely answered her question: 'How much do you love me?'" I perceive.

As I gaze upon the extinguished fire in the stove, the embers cast a soft glow, their warmth enveloping me like a comforting embrace on this chilly winter morning. The gentle crackle of the remaining embers invites me to linger in their embrace a moment longer. Outside, the morning chorus of roosters echoes through the quiet dawn, their calls a reminder of the new day dawning. I watch as a faint twilight begins to paint the sky, heralding the arrival of a new day filled with possibilities and opportunities. In this tranquil moment, surrounded by the remnants of warmth and the promise of a new beginning, I find solace in the quiet beauty of the morning, hoping for the simple joys that the new day brings.